ANGELOS ODYSSEY

VOLUME FIVE

BY

J. B. M. PATRICK

SHINGEN BLUE PUBLISHING

OREGON

Published in the United States of America

First Edition

Shingen Blue Publishing

Oregon

This is a work of fiction. Names, characters, businesses, places, events and incidents are either the products of the author's imagination or used in a fictitious manner. Any resemblance to actual persons, living or dead, or actual events is purely coincidental.

ISBN: 978-1-7353379-1-3

"For education among all kinds of men always has had, and always will have, an element of danger and revolution, of dissatisfaction and discontent."

— *W. E. B. Du Bois*

CONTENTS

-

PART ONE: The Swarm — 7

-

1 – The Armada: 9

--

PART TWO: Brock — 17

--

1 – Enrec: 19
2 – Class: 29
3 – Squad Tactics: 35
4 – Team Exercise: 43
5 – Solidarity: 59
6 – Private Ronas: 77
7 – Room Clearing: 81
8 – Despair: 99
9 – Breaking: 115
10 – Disassociation: 135
11 – The Last Chamber: 145
12 – Stepping Forward: 153

Note From The Author — 160

For

Everyone

We're on our way to Saizakune. Everything I need to know about my target, about Guin, will be made clear. I can't forget that this all ends in death. I've got a dark mountain to climb.

PART ONE
The Swarm

1
The Armada

-

Tavon

-

WE'RE AMIDST THE CLOUDS, aboard an aircraft that's over a hundred miles from its destination. All around is silence. In the deep blue sky, underneath the bright Sun, we drift along in the silence, hurrying toward the end.

In the blink of an eye, I notice three black specks suddenly appear in the distance while I look out the window of the interior of a lounge lit by daylight. Another blink, and there's seven more of them, like dark wasps that inch closer and closer.

Baraka Williams takes out a white talisman from his left sleeve, presses his palms together over it, and says, "May I have eyes without a body and a presence which can't be seen."

White tau washes over Baraka in a wave that dissolves his form before splashing into the ground at his feet; a vibrant concentration of energy gathers around the spot on the floor where he vanished, and then it whisks itself away.

When I glance out of the window again, as Kagiso, Raiko, and Hadrian all collectively gasp in confusion, I can see a growing storm of black. Without blinking, I watch as dark spheres form on the horizon and then converge before expanding outward into shapes too far away to distinguish from one another.

"Yo!" Raiko nudges Hadrian, who shoulders him angrily and shouts back, "I'm already looking, idiot! Baraka—"

Hadrian look toward where Baraka disappeared and calls after him, "I know you're still here! What's going on?"

Kagiso becomes pale and hunches over. "Dammit. I didn't think this would happen so soon."

"What are you talking about," Hadrian demands, "speak up!"

Kagiso tries to look at him but trembles and looks away as he replies, "We're not in any recognized jurisdiction right now. They've got us."

"Who's got us?" Raiko exclaims.

"The Maeja."

Every second, more and more wasps appear and draw nearer. When they're close enough, I can see wide, spike-helmed aircrafts soaring our way; feathery, life-like wings extend from both sides, and blue flames are evoked from their exhaust systems. Each aircraft's exterior is designed in much the same way, with white, narrow pipes wrapped around them in groves placed next to white latticing which resembles the connections on a microchip.

A swarm of black ships closes in and encircles our vessel, which is more than twice the size of a single one of them. In spite of that, everyone's looking out of whatever window they can in dreadful anticipation.

I stand up from my seat and ask Kagiso, "What do they want?"

"It's not about what they can do for us. It's about what we can do for them," he says.

I feel a burst of adrenaline cause my body to shake as a wave of aura forces its way through the interior of our ship. Several distinct concentrations of zol emit pressure from different spots throughout the lounge.

Human silhouettes are seemingly scanned into existence, appearing as ink-black heads that grow dark bodies beneath them. Like the fading of a flame, the darkness obscuring their true forms dissipates beneath the colors of blue, grey, and brown blazers overtop white undershirts.

As suited strangers appear all around us, Kagiso finally elaborates:

"The Maeja are a crew that goes around kidnapping people. They're slavers." He stares at me wide-eyed and says, "I... forgot about them."

Another dark form appears to my right. A man with short dreads and who's rocking an all-tan suit with no undershirt emerges; he turns to look past us, exposing the tattoo of what looks like a fanged owl with the body of a snake on his chest, and he grins while studying another group of travelers seated around the table next to us.

"Heh," he chuckles and says, "good morning. What a perfect day to die on."

He draws a semiauto pistol and shoots each of his victims in the head with one controlled spray of bullets. The shooter aims at the next table and yells, "Get on the ground!"—he points the barrel of his weapon at different groups and repeats—"Get on the fucking ground!"

When one passenger stalls for too long, he fires six rounds into his body and chuckles again before more casually ordering everyone to get down again. But, even as they obey him, other Maeja gunners take on the same attitude as this guy and shoot a few passengers of their own, laughing all the while.

Still more of them are teleporting in. As soon as they appear, they begin using stun guns and electric batons to corral everyone within the same area. Most of them comply, and yet they pile on more abuse, beating on anyone who doesn't move fast enough or for no reason at all.

I rush toward the tattooed slaver and channel Jeigon as quickly as I can.

A long set of chain-links flashes before my eyes, then—

They smack against my chest hard enough to tear at my skin. I feel incredible force pull me off balance, and I barely manage to stop myself from falling onto my ass. Even as I recover, Hadrian appears at my side, wraps the chain-links around me once more, and then tries to lock me in place.

"Hey! What the hell are you doing?"

When I look back at Hadrian, all I can see is terror clear across his features.

Raiko approaches Hadrian from behind while balling up his fists, but Hadrian says to him, "Stop. We can't fight them."

"What?" Raiko shouts, "Sure we can—what are you doing?"

Kagiso puts his hand on Raiko's shoulder and nods. "He's right. It's not worth it."

"Well, well," the tattooed stranger looks us over with a smile, "*that* was unexpected. A Hayashi capturing a human? How'd you pull that off so well, huh?"

"I wanted to impress the Maeja."

"Wait, what?" Raiko asks him.

"Raiko, shut up!" I shout back to keep him from getting shot.

Several of the gunmen circle us while also condensing the victims they've gathered into one spot. Kagiso and Raiko are separated and ordered to kneel on the ground while Hadrian and I remain where we are. From out of the corner of my left eye, I see a familiar face being led my way alongside a much younger companion.

Artemis Spilsbury and Avodeus are brought into the lounge area from the hallway outside, and the three of us immediately make eye contact.

"All right then," the one with the semiautomatic nods his head, looks at Hadrian, and replies, "we'll take the help if you're good enough. How strong are you?"

"Strong enough to be a member of Noboros. Is that what you're looking for?"

"If it's the same 'Noboros' that I'm thinking of…" he says with a smile and strokes his goatee, "then that might make you overqualified. Ha!"

He grins wickedly at Hadrian. "Are you sure you want to be a pirate? We all die young, you know."

"I've made up my mind already. This human's skilled at fighting, so I thought I'd trade him for a place among you."

"Hmm. A Hayashi slaver… I never would've thought."

Hadrian reassures him, "I want to rob as many humans as I can. They'll experience a new level of misery if you let me help you."

It feels like a waste to do nothing. They've been shooting people for little other reason than entertainment, and it's pissing me off. I can take this stupid bandit—I can feel the strength surging through me now! That's right, I'll break these chains and handle them all by myself.

I clench my fists and step toward my opponent.

Artemis grabs my arm. His thoughts briefly reach out to mine through Imago; he says, *"Don't move."*

The gunman behind Artemis rams his elbow into the Death Officer's back and then shoves him forward. At the same moment, another Maeja pirate shouts at the semiautomatic-wielder in front of me: "Titus! The boss wants to see you now!"

Before Titus can react to my outburst, he instantly becomes quiet while peering into the crowd of gunmen surrounding 'the boss.' Toward the western end of the room, I turn to see a strange-looking human who appears to be over ten feet tall. The top half of his body is hunched over; his neck is abnormally thick and angles inward while pressing out broad, convoluted veins. The face of Titus' boss is somewhat contorted to the side and bloated, with two vertical eyes that look past anything they happen to stare at and no discernible expression behind a thin, dark shroud of zol covering his entire body.

When 'the boss' moves, he limps forward tiredly, but each step he takes resounds with considerable weight. Titus almost takes a step back when looking upon the giant, but he swallows and bows at the waist out of respect.

"Boss, one of the passengers wishes to join us," he announces.

The tall abomination twists his entire neck to stare at me and Hadrian with an empty look, then he looks back at Titus. He reaches out at him with one index finger, and tau the color of grey sludge spirals around it.

Titus' own zol extends out around his body and intercepts his boss's aura, but grime and a liquid substance, congealed in some parts, infiltrates the barrier. The tau of his boss spreads like an infection and begins to obscure Titus with dark blue ulcers that grow and grow.

"Sygdom, stop!" Titus cries out. "I can't—I can't—"

His boss withdraws his hand, and the aura projected from him soars forward, past Titus like a wave of energy, and dissipates behind him. All of Sygdom's disgusting ability spreads out into the air we breathe, and I start to cough. As everyone else around me erupts into violent coughing fits, the Maeja begin cursing, screaming at us to, "Shut the fuck up!"

Like before, they start firing on people and mocking them. "CEASE."

Sygdom's voice carries with it a noxious cloud, one which fills the room again with an awful odor. This time some of the Maeja begin to cough as well, but most stiffen and watch with apprehension. Sygdom turns his neck to look back at Titus; when he speaks, it's like a throaty bellow, and he inhales deep before saying to him, "Your immunity has grown, my friend."

Sygdom looks out into the crowd of Maeja thugs and asks, "Is Vishok present?"

"Over here, boss!"

From the entrance to the lounge, a tall human ducks down to pass through and drags a double-bladed axe behind him. He's only got on a pair of jeans; when he stands up straight, I see tattoos of animals, peoples' faces, symbols, and writing in different languages covering the entire top half of his body. Vishok wears the horned skull of a beast over his head like a visor; it's decorated with a yellow mane, and blood runs down from his mouth to cover most of his chest and stomach. Behind his axe, I see a trail of red.

He's eager to see Sygdom, but, when he takes notice of me and Hadrian, he brandishes his axe and snarls.

"You want me to take care of them, big boss?"

"No, no," Sygdom replies while beckoning him forward, "come here. I need to see something."

Vishok lets his axe drop to the ground as he strides forward and then kneels before Sygdom.

"Titus' immunity has shown improvement. I want to see yours now."

He touches Vishok's forehead before the warrior can protect himself...

Vishok starts to shake and grunts prior to grinding his teeth. His face flushes red and then purple as thick sludge washes over him. Vishok twitches uncontrollably as his body seems to shrink inward.

"Boss..." he begs, "it's—it's too much..."

"Hmph." Sygdom snorts derisively and then turns away from him to address Titus again, "He's all talk and no show. I expected better. After today, Titus will serve as my second-in-command, as he is the only one who can stand to be around me."

"But boss," Titus points at us and asks, "we've got another fighter on our hands. A Hayashi captured a human to impress us, and he says that he wants to join the crew in exchange for his good deed."

"Is that so?" Sygdom studies me with the same lack of emotion as before, and then...

He bares sharp, crooked teeth in a smile that stretches from ear to ear. His grin pronounces the narrowness of his head; he begins to drool.

"Wonderful. But it would be a waste to simply expose him to my ability."

Vishok struggles to stand again and breathes in hard as he interjects, "I'll fight him! None of these other weaklings stood a chance against me, so let me have a go at him, boss!"

Sygdom extends his index finger toward Vishok, and Vishok flinches while taking a few steps back; Sygdom smiles.

"That would also be a waste, Vishok. As of now, you're in a weakened state, and I can't be sure that a stranger won't try to deceive you and end the fight before it has even begun.

"No..." Sygdom groans while looking over the victims the Maeja have gathered.

"Big boss!"

An older man with long, grey hair pushes Artemis forward to stand next to me.

"This freak cut down some of our guys earlier. He only stopped and came quietly when we ganged up on him, so he's probably got plenty of fight left in him!"

"They're both Death Officers," Hadrian chimes in.

"Very good," Sygdom nods with a look of grotesque pleasure. "Two Death Officers should provide more than enough entertainment for everyone.

"How about this," he taunts Artemis and I and says, "the two of you will fight to the death. If the victor can kill his opponent in under five minutes, then he'll be set free. If you go over... well, that would be very boring to the Maeja. Entertain us. Give it everything you've got. Kill each other."

PART TWO
Brock

1
Enrec

--

Brock

--

I'M ABOARD A GIANT, oval aircraft that's painted the color of blue steel. Along with five hundred strangers, I'm sitting within one of several rows of black, leather seats. Directly in front of us all, we see the holographic projection of a soldier dressed in combat gear. The soldier sits with his palms flat against his lower thighs and with his back upright, with instructions in bold letters above reading: "Correct your posture accordingly."

Outside the long, horizontal window panels around us, I catch a glimpse of the Lower-City of the Citadel as we make our descent into the World Below. It looks peaceful from where I'm sitting, but we've lost at least one-third of our country. On the insides of its walls, there's no one left who I can help. Not yet.

A deep, electronic hum reverberates throughout the interior. Steel panels slide to cover the windows and darken the room. The image of the soldier disappears; all that's left behind is a white void, and a man steps into the light. He's wearing a fitted, navy coat with matching dress pants. His shaved head exposes a broad scar running along the side of it, and he's got on an eyepatch which covers his right eye.

This man looks us all over with a solemn expression. His neck twitches every few seconds. It twitches harder when he finally chooses to speak.

"Everyone understands why they're here today, and so I won't waste anyone's time. My name is Modukai Sergeant Kupha, and you've all agreed to the same contract. You belong to Enrec, which itself is being managed by the Democratic Council for the time being. The sentinels we had programmed to defend our outposts were stolen from us by the Dawn Bureau, and so the Citadel's entire goddamned army has been spread thin protecting whatever parts of our country it can. Without Enrec, we're finished."

Kupha's face reddens as he twitches more frequently and begins to raise his voice, "They want me to give you guys the 'hero's speech,' the cleaned-up version of what the reality of your job is. I'm going to tell you the truth, all right? Once I've told you this, the indoctrination process can begin...

"Everyone here is going to be broken down, changed, and made into professional killers. Your jobs are to go over to Alandran settlements, engage with the enemy, and skullfuck them into submission. Do you understand?"

The room erupts as everyone shouts, "YES SERGEANT!"

"Today you'll be joining the biggest gang in the Republic of Avva. We've moved our bases of operation farther Southeast, and, when we land, you'll enter a unique training program that will keep you separate from the main body of our army. All of this follows a natural process; just trust in the system, listen to the people who outrank you, and you'll adapt without a problem.

"After you've all been conditioned for the upcoming operation, you'll specialize in reconnaissance training, and that's why you're being paid more than people at my own rank. To be frank, all of you will see combat. If you fall in combat, the Republic will be delivering fat checks to your families in recognition of your sacrifices. This private battalion is going to consist of the strongest soldiers in the country. Be bold and learn as much as possible. It'll make the difference between life and death."

"YES SERGEANT!"

Kupha laughs and says, "If you make it out alive, who knows, you might just end up like me. I was a part of the last recon unit, and now they're all gone."

He smirks.

"I wish you all the best of luck. If you see the Devil, shoot him in the face."

--

Our destination's deep within the narrow peaks of dark, sand-colored mountains, where at least twenty separate outposts have been established. Now that the window panels have been exposed again, I can see that each outpost is marked by desert-tan domes that could easily be missed from a distance and are mostly obscured by mountain ridges. This location is a few hour's flight from the Citadel and a mostly uninhabited area belonging to the World Below. Enrec has constructed a solitary network here which can monitor events in both the Citadel and its surrounding territories, but its primary purpose is to make a move on Alandra.

As our airship moves in closer, I can just make out formations of soldiers dressed in camouflaged outfits in shades of tan and brown. We pass over octagonal domes connected to buildings of similar shapes, patches filled with glass greenhouses and energy generators, and automated mechs of various sizes.

Our assigned outpost, Echo-14, is tucked away in the southmost area and far from the rest of the main body of Enrec's army in the World Below. A plateau graces the base of a short mountain overlooking the dunes that wind and stretch across the landscape ahead. A pale dome sticks out from the center of the plateau and is connected by a tube encased in white steel to a smaller, circular building. This is where we'll be receiving our training.

But, instead of actually landing on the plateau, we're taken down the side of it, where a dirt trails leads down into the bowels of a dark basin. The airship descends to the bottom of it, and Modukai General Kupha starts to speak again:

"All right, warriors. This'll be the first challenge, and it's going to break a lot of people.

"Once you step off this aircraft, you'll be handed a duffel bag. It's going to be heavy as shit, and you're going to carry this bag all the way up the trail and create a proper formation out of those who make it. You'll do this in under thirty minutes, and, if you so much as fucking dare to fail, you'll be sent back home and charged for the expenses you incurred for wasting our time, plus interest. Does everyone understand?"

"YES SERGEANT!"

"Let's go," he orders.

Kupha leads us to the back and lowest area of the plane, where we wait as a steel platform descends to touch the ground and create a bridge onto the land below it. Once it does, the Modukai Sergeant barks at us to move, shouting, "Go! Go! Go!"

I'm out of the exit with the rest of them, sprinting into the light—

A duffel bag hits me in the head.

I fall on my back and just as another Sergeant screams in my face, "Get the fuck up, dumbass! We don't have all fucking day!"

I smell the alcohol on his breath as I come to stand and strap the bag to my back—

He kicks me in the side, and, with rage, I charge forward, ignoring him completely. I keep my distance from any other Sergeants I see while proceeding up the path, and angry shouts echo around me. I climb the first slope preceding several more, and there I see another recruit being pushed off to start all over again. I rush past the Sergeant who pushed him, and he calls after me, "Pussy! Why don't you come protect him? Don't you want him for yourself—don't you want to make him your bitch?"

I avoid confrontation and sprint, weaving around clusters of runners as I pass them up. When I can't seem to get by a larger group of recruits, someone from behind shoves me into the person in front of me, and I accidentally knock him down while trying to stop myself from tripping. He curses at me as I regain my balance, but a steel canister striking the ground between us catches everyone off guard. It explodes, producing white smoke behind me and sending up gasps from the recruits at my back; at the same time, I hear the sound of rifles being fired into the air, and they drown out the voices of the Sergeants below.

I move up onto the third slope, where yet another Sergeant intercepts me with a kick to the gut. I keel over but move forward in spite of the pain, and he steps in close to push me off my feet.

"Why the fuck are you moving so slow, dude? Huh? What's the problem—do you want to go home?"

I get to my feet, try to move ahead, and this asshole kicks me in the shin.

"You wanna fight me and go to jail, newbie? C'mon, try me!"

He grabs my arm, pulls me toward himself to throw me off balance, and—

Another recruit plows into him. The Sergeant falls on his face, and the guy who helped me gives me a pat on the back before charging onward and shouting, "You can thank me later!"

Seeing him move ahead with confidence rubs off on me. I detach my mind from my body. I remove myself from any feelings of pain or exhaustion, and I follow behind him.

After ascending a few more levels, most everyone slows into one pack of runners. Shouting continues to echo from below, but my breathing's louder than anything else. Every muscle in my body tightens; I'm close to overheating. The Sun beams down through the dust-filled skies above. Sweat gets in my eyes, and it burns so much that I can barely see my way up.

I was enlisted before, so I understand how to cope. I'm not the best, but I'm far ahead of most of our battalion by now. As my running slows, more recruits pass me here and there. Just when I start to speed up, the guy who helped me before begins slowing down so that we meet again along the way. On the rest of the way up, I run side-by-side with a man around my age, except he's got a full head of long, brown hair and an overgrown beard. Because we're such a "unique" unit, typical appearance regulations don't really apply to us; as long as we survive, we're surpassing expectations.

"What's your name, guy?" he managers to utter in between panting.

"Brock."

"Brock? All right. I'm Horokaida."

"Good to meet you," I reply in between harsh, shallow breaths, "and good looking out."

"Of course," he says. "We've got to work together if we're going to get through this."

--

After a quiet, agonizing trek along the rest of the trail, Horokaida and I arrive at the top of the plateau.

Outside of the main domed enclosure, which shines white from the rays of the Sun, a dozen recruits have gathered into a loose formation in front of four different instructors dressed in camouflaged vests with plate carriers attached to them. Each one of them wields black rifles that have holographic scopes and a long, broad barrels. Each one stands stoically in place, repeating the same instructions: "Take out the black beret from your duffel bag and put it on, then rezip your bag and place it to your right. Line up into rows of thirty and make fifteen columns out of your formation."

Their instructions are simple, but, once I've opened my bag, finding a beret among what looks like thirty different tools and pieces of clothing is harder than it sounds. To make matters worse, the four Sergeants suddenly cut our time shorter.

"If all four hundred and fifty of you don't get into proper formation within the next five minutes, we'll have to punish you. If the person standing next to you is fucked up, then you're fucked up."

Horokaida and I both rummage desperately through our belongings and manage to find our berets not long after we're given our orders. Unfortunately for us, most of our unit hasn't reached the plateau yet. We've got two minutes left, and everyone around us is in different states of readiness. While at least a hundred recruits gather into formation and find out what's going on, our time begins to run out before even half of our battalion's caught up.

The Sergeants at the front count down, "Five. Four. Three…"

The woman next to me finds her beret and sighs as she says, "They're being petty."

One of the vested Sergeants screams, "Stop! Everybody stop!"

The plateau is filled with a momentary silence before he fires several rounds into the air and thunders, "I am Modukai Sergeant Onaem, the Senior Instructor of this unit.

"I gave you all a very easy task, was generous with the time given, and you all fucked it up. You fucked it up so badly that the Citadel might just be doomed because of little ignorant weaklings like you. How about you all have some fucking discipline—" Onaem points at us and screams, "everyone start doing pushups, but forget about cadence. Do *perfect* pushups as fast as you can. If your form slacks at all, one of the Modai Sergeants here will kindly beat your ass into obedience. Do it NOW," he demands, and everyone obeys.

Simultaneously, the other three sergeants carrying assault rifles spring into action. They begin shouting at people who don't move quickly enough and kick others who fail to demonstrate perfect form. All the while, Onaem continues lecturing us:

"Every recon unit Enrec has is an experiment, and you're just the suicidal dummies who decided to sign up for it. The world would laugh if they could see you now. But don't worry, recruits, we're all going with you. That's why we have to make sure that you're ready. Everybody, stand back up."

We do as instructed, and Onaem says, "You've got five minutes to get your berets and gather into a proper formation. Hurry up."

By now, hundreds of recruits have made it to the top of the plateau. In spite of our swelling numbers, though, the stragglers prevent us from achieving a formation that's four hundred and fifty soldiers strong and uniform. When Onaem starts to count down again, those at the top of the plateau begin cursing at the recruits trying to catch up down below.

They don't make it in time, and Onaem proceeds to have us do ab workouts in sync; when we get too tired for that, he switches us back to pushups; when pushups wear everyone down even more, he orders us to run laps around the main building.

It ends soon after that, and, once again, he gives us another time limit. "Three minutes," he tells us.

Three minutes, and only half of us have got on our berets.

"I don't think they'll be so merciful this time," the woman to my left says.

When I turn to look at her, I see that she's about as broad-shouldered as I am. She's got stark white hair cut into a bob which falls around a beautiful face, with bright green eyes staring back at me from behind narrow, rimless glasses.

"No matter what they put us through," I reply, "we can adapt."

"You think so?" she asks.

We run out of time again.

"Stop! Everybody stop where you are," cries Onaem.

At that moment, the last member of our unit makes it to the top with the help of two other recruits. Four hundred and fifty of us are now where we need to be, but only a little over half are dressed and positioned appropriately.

Onaem loses his temper.

"All right, all right," he shouts, "new plan, okay? Those of you who've been squared away can stay put. As for everyone else, gather together to the left of the formation—NOW!"

Anyone who isn't already "squared away" parts from our formation and murmurs confusedly as they come together into a group of mixed errors.

"Shut the fuck up!" Onaem yells at them, and they go silent while staring back at the sergeant in a loose group.

"There are two types of people here today: winners and quitters. The quitters don't give a fuck about anyone else but themselves—they're selfish. Hey, everybody who did the right thing, tell them that they're selfish quitters."

The formation around me repeats what he says, but I stay silent. Onaem continues:

"Selfish quitters are very taxing to the State. It's these losers who will go home to flirt with your wives, collect taxpayer dollars, and burden our failing economy. They want to go home, so we'll go die for them so that they can do that. Isn't that right, quitters? You want to go home?"

Most of them remain silent, but a couple here and there shake their heads in denial.

"You want to go home, don't you?" another sergeant asks while coming to stand at Onaem's side.

"It's okay. You can say it," yet another chimes in as they approach.

All four sergeants stare at the disorganized group with blank expressions.

"We're giving you an out," Onaem says in a low voice, "that's why you didn't make it on time. It's because you don't want to be here, but that's okay. You want to go home, so let's send them home, boys. Are you ready?"

"Wait! Wait!" members of the group raise their hands and cry out, "We'll stay!" They plead, "Don't shoot!"

"Welcome home, parasites."

All four of them shoot into the crowd. From behind, five more sergeants close off any routes of escape, then they fire upon the rest of the recruits who they've rejected.

Next to their idea of a "perfect formation," the fallen lie dead all around us.

2
Class

--

Brock

--

"THIS IS DAY ONE OF YOUR TRAINING,"
Modukai Sergeant Onaem tells us from behind a
wooden desk. "In about a week, your training will
be completed. Don't ask us when it will be; we don't know. If
the government decides that it needs troops now, then we
could deploy as early as tomorrow."

Three more Modukai Sergeants sit next to Onaem and
shuffle through holographic paperwork on desks of their own.
Onaem is the only person in authority with a five o' clock
shadow, and his dark blue bangs hang over a set of grey, piercing eyes. To his left is Modai Sergeant Kusinon, and Modai
Sergeants Vladik and Bach begin glaring at the remaining four
hundred and ten of us. Above Onaem's head, a green, plexi-
glass screen emits holographic code sequences that vanish and
then reappear to merge and form a broad view of the Cities of
Alandra.

From the projection, I can see walled citadels built along
an archipelago consisting of hundreds of small islands. Each
major municipality has white and diamond-colored towers that
reach far into the clouds; above the collection of cities, cargo
cruisers abound in the skies and pass between the hangar bays
attached to larger trading stations suspended in the air.

"Alandra is the second-greatest trade empire in the world,
the first being the Lokanic Republic of the Gods. Everyone
here knows what the Citadel's been through. We no longer
have the same political power as Alandra, and the traffic on
our trade routes is starting to dwindle down to nothing. While
our enemies are enjoying peace in the South, the airship foundations keeping our nation in the sky are running out of fuel."

Onaem abruptly stands, and his face reddens like before as
he shouts, "They've taken advantage of us! When the Gozadalus Cult attacked, Alandra sent guerilla forces to strike where

we least expected confrontation. These privileged Alandran assholes don't have to worry about their families falling from the sky and being smashed into the fucking ground! Over there, they talk about 'equality.' They accept everyone, human and nonhuman, but they don't give a shit about you. No."

Modai Sergeant Kusinon touches a small, glass pad, and the image above flashes and changes into the picture of a machine that looks a lot like a sentinel. It's not as bulky in its frame; in fact, black wires cover a slender, grey body with navy-blue metal cuffs, polygonal, metallic hands, and an empty face with an eye like the barrel of a gun.

"The name of your unit is Echo-14: The Okehazama Battalion. Everyone in this room is the *fourteenth* recon team that Enrec has assembled. We started with brigade-sized units, and, as each one of them was wiped out, the soldiers sent to us came in smaller numbers. The last few recon units before you were nearly all killed in action much faster than anyone expected…"

Onaem points to the image and says, "All because of the weapons they've been deploying against us. What you see above me is called an 'E-Drone.' Not only can it shoot you in the face with the automatic rounds it fires from its hands, but the Alandran military's been rigging them to explode whenever they get close enough to engage with our soldiers. They've been mass producing these things, with less of a focus on how durable they might be and more on how much damage they can deal.

"Along with these bastards,"—he sighs just as Kusinon triggers the next slide to reveal a mech suit designed for the average human body as well as a silver tank pictured below it—"you'll have to contend with human and nonhuman combatants as well. Alandra makes use of much of the same equipment as us, and so, recruits, we expect you to overcome humans, nonhumans, combat drones, and, unfortunately, *demons.*"

The room becomes eerily silent, and Onaem nods his head. "I'm not talking out of my ass when I say this, but use of demons on the battlefield is a tactic they've started employing more recently. We don't know what works against them; it's different every time, and they've been getting worse. The Republic of Avva has a few cities a little ways Northwest of here, and, so far, most of our efforts have gone toward protecting them from whatever Alandra sends our way."

Onaem slams his fist on the table, screaming, "They WANT to kill all of us. Do you understand? Do you?"

"YES SERGEANT!" we all shout in unison.

He bangs his fist on the table again and says, "Perfect. There's a reason why we eliminated the most disobedient of you. Every operation before this one has just been fucking practice,"—Onaem throws his hands up in the air nonchalantly—"practice that's turned into skirmishes with Alandran inbred scum, and, each time, those fuckers took more than we could give.

"The Okehazama Brigade's gonna change that. Everything that you're about to learn is going to prepare you for the first invasion this country has conducted in a long time."

Gasps go up all around, and, as people start to whisper to each other, Kusinon screams, "Shut the fuck up! No one said to talk—did anyone say that? No. Shut the fuck up and listen to the people who outrank you."

Onaem proceeds without paying us any attention, "We know, through what intelligence we've gathered, that Alandra plans to attack the Citadel within the near future, and so Enrec has developed a countertactic to give the main body of our soldiers more time to push back the Cult of Gozadalus. Echo-14 is the most important group of warriors in the country at the moment, and that's why we're going with you on this mission.

"It's all or nothing, everyone. The building you're in right now is just a classroom. There are no beds here, and the majority of this facility is underground. Show them, Sergeant Kusinon."

He obliges, and the screen above changes to show a map overlay of the area below the domed shelter. From the classroom, a passage, outlined in bright blue, descends down into a network of longer passages that extend far enough to connect with tunnels from the closest outposts. This giant network looks like dozens of neon blue pipes scattered in all directions, big enough to contain a small city.

"For almost a decade, the Okehazama Project has staggered toward completion. The tunnels you see are made out of mezatonicum and netite; the mezatonicum generates its own gravitational field that pushes outward, and the netite lining the inside of the network of tunnels expands it into three times its normal size.

"This is where we conduct our training operations. Also, the use of a chemical in mezatonicum, atonicylate, makes excavation easier for our drilling squads. Because of that chemical, we've made some progress in the direction of Alandra, and many of the battalions before you were able to set up camps that we've tried to convert into underground outposts for the ongoing war. For now, you'll be going with us to the start of the network.

"We don't have time to properly train any of you, but, Avva willing, we'll do our best."

--

An elevator embedded with netite and the size of a small fortress accommodates everyone in Unit Echo-14 before taking us down into the tunnels. In the middle of the recruits, nine Enrec Sergeants stand with their backs to each other and appear to brood silently as it gets darker around everyone.

We descend into pitch black and then blinding white that softens into a shining blue. We're lowered into a room of white tiles that are outlined by neon squares of light and enter a massive chamber which ends in groups of tunnel entrances in every cardinal direction.

"Let's go!" Onaem shouts while charging ahead and leading the other sergeants behind him. "The faster you understand what it is you're going to be doing, the more of a handle you'll get on what's to come."

Onaem takes us to the western end of the chamber and stops in front of a series of netite doors running along the wall. Each one is an opaque, dark blue, with small windows that look like they lead into the open sky.

"Listen up, newbies," Onaem says to us, "you're all going to break up into, as close as possible, thirty squads of fifteen and choose one door out of the thirty-five available to you. Only one squad per door. You'll navigate as far as the first camp you see. Since you've all made it this far and know that there's no going back, we can explain a little of what's going on out there before you get started. Once you're in, though, you're all on your own."

Onaem clears his throat and continues with a calm, even tone, "The Democratic Council have given their consent to a premature attack on Alandra's forward operating bases in the South. Enrec is going to use the full might of its forces to strike at our oldest enemy, and what we're called upon to do from there will make all the difference.

"For the time being, however, all of you will be put through a training circuit which should quickly familiarize you with everything that you need to know about the enemy. From this chamber, we'll monitor your progress and give you instructions wherever necessary. Other than that," he says with a smirk, "you're going to learn the value of teamwork very quickly. If everyone's ready, let's recite the Creed of the Republic, swear our allegiances to this great nation, and strike terror into the hearts of the motherfuckers who dare to point their guns at us."

--

Right after the recital of the Creed, which involves me repeating how much I love and want to fight for the Republic, some people begin studying one another with both confusion and apprehension. Others form groups faster and start to gather outside of different doors, gossiping about "lucky numbers" as they try to choose the right passage.

Sergeant Kusinon screams, "It's not fucking speed dating—choose somebody who you think will keep you from getting shot! Hurry the fuck up!"

Horokaida and I nod to each other, and the white-haired woman from before approaches us with a smile and bows politely. We do the same in return, and she says to us, "My name's Ein Bira. Is it all right if I join you guys? You seem… mellow."

"Sure. I've done this all before, so it should be easy," I reply with a nod.

"So have I," says Horokaida.

"Veterans, huh?" a new voice interrupts us.

A short man with curly, brown hair and a robust body approaches with a taller but skinnier stranger who has grey hair and a grizzly, black beard. The shorter man reaches his hand out to me and introduces himself, "My name's Hannibal Martin. You wanna team up with us?"

"Sure," I reply and shake his hand, then I meet the eyes of the other stranger before shaking his.

"Fichte Evans," he says.

When others take notice of the small group forming around the five of us, it rapidly swells to the number of fifteen. In a second, we're ready to choose a door, and, because no one's feeling superstitious, we arbitrarily pick number ten.

I grab the door's metal handle, turn it, and lead us into the great passage beyond the portal.

3
Squad Tactics

--

Brock

--

"THIS IS MODUKAI SERGEANT ONAEM," a voice seems to reverberate from the ceiling far above us, "if you can hear me, then *now* is the time to inspect your gear. We're only going to give you this tutorial once. First, take out the black robe in your duffel bag; I'll give you exactly a minute to find it."

Rather than any normal-sized hallway, we've crossed to the other side to find a sprawling expanse of white tiles and odd-looking formations jutting out of them in some spots like mountains of marble. There's more than enough space for the fifteen of us to lay out our equipment, and getting this damn bag off my shoulders for once feels like I'm dropping a boulder that I've been carrying all this way.

Ein and Horokaida stay close by as they unzip their duffel bags. Other than those two, Hannibal is the only other member of our squad who doesn't mind standing near us. The rest introduced themselves earlier, but I'm still struggling to get their names straight.

Overhead, Onaem starts counting down, "Five. Four…"

I find a thick garment buried beneath a gun case and a series of wire and then hold it up to make sure that it matches what everyone else has.

Onaem explains: "We've given you what's called a *Zega Robe*. The bundles of wires in your bags need to be threaded through openings in the robe, as special sections of it are made of netite. These robes are strong enough to withstand bullets, and they've got ammo pouches sewn into them. You've got three minutes to get dressed, to thread the *Ethernic Cable* through your robes, and to retrieve the gas masks and helmets out of your bags."

The four of us quickly shuffle through our gear, and my hands close around what feels like flexible steel. I pull a grey helmet out of my duffel bag and examine its black visor before rummaging through my stuff again to grab onto the rubber face-seal of a dirty, olive-green gas mask. The smell of earth and mildew fills the air as everyone begins dumping their equipment out to make the search easier.

"You'll have to remove your helmet in order to wear the gas mask, but, with the helmet on, the Ethernic Cable provides you with its full protection. Now, store your gas masks somewhere you'll remember and put on your helmets. The power of the netite wrapped around your bodies won't last forever, so try not to get hit."

In between Onaem's instructions, and after donning my helmet, I start to shiver. Sharp, sudden pain digs at the back of my neck and then burns hot with an awful sensation that runs down my entire back. Scorching heat radiates into my arms and legs; Ein and Horokaida both cry out, and this prompts me to look in their direction.

A dozen small needles impale the backs of their necks and extend into their bodies, like they have into mine, and most everyone stiffens at once.

"What the hell?" Horokaida exclaims.

"Must be to protect us," says Hannibal while looking over his outfit. "It feels... tighter, like I won't be able to take it off."

Onaem orders from up above, "Set your food rations, water canteens, medic kits, ammo, and gas masks to the side. The next few items are some of the most important.

"First, the white metal shoes in your bags have propulsion jets installed within them. They'll enable you to cover long distances at a rapid rate, but don't use them if you're right next to each other.

"Next, there's a piece of netite that you should all have. Keep this safe and remember it for later.

"All of you should also have at least one grenade. After that, set aside the *Maia Technical Handbook*, and then each one of you should be left with either one or more unique weapons. We weren't able to provide equal sets of equipment for everyone because we've been slowly running out with each iteration of recruits.

"Soldiers, you are the last reconnaissance unit that Enrec will be capable of training for a long time. Because of how important this mission is, Enrec's repurposed a lot of the Alandran drones we've captured in order to give you a good idea of what it's like to face off with them. Fortunately for you, and since you're all newbies, we've given these repurposed bots weak points and deficiencies that should be marked for you in the early sections of this maze. As you go farther in… well…

"Our mission is twofold, people. While we train, we make progress. We don't always know how much of the tunnels have been compromised by Alandran forces at any point. The mezatonicum keeps them from just outright fucking bombing it, and so they've chosen to fuck with us using our own network. This is the world you're about to be a part of, everyone.

"If you think that we can go about this nicely, then you're wrong and you could get somebody hurt. We want killers. That's all we care about. So, if you're not going to go out there and do as much damage as possible, then die early on for the sake of our time, got it? Good. Now, hurry up and get to the first campsite. You've got an hour."

After strapping on the heaviest boots I've ever worn, I look through my bag one more time to see what "unique weapon" these bastards are talking about.

I feel a heatwave come over me. I'm caught off guard, and I look over at Jean-Pierre Sato, another of our squad members, who presses in on the sides of a wide, silver disk and causes the contraption to contract. A sword springs out from a narrow, blocky handle, and small grooves within both sides of the blade seethe with bright flames.

A dark, corroded form abruptly appears behind him. Some wretched creature hunches over Jean-Pierre. Its head's misshaped, dented on one side and pointed on the other; its face is stretched too far upward and into a permanent sullen expression, with empty sockets for eyes that can see more than they should. This monster has the head of a botched scarecrow and the body of a minotaur, but, instead of hands, its arms end in two black spikes.

It shoves one spike through Jean-Pierre's chest and forces its entire arm through him as a volley of blood shoots forward from the strike! The monster withdraws its arm and vanishes—

It appears behind me, its face hovering right next to my ear.

The demon says, *"It's not fair. Your army has kept me waiting for too long. Alandra got to have all the fun."*

I turn, prepared to swing on the devil, but there's no one behind me. I hear his voice again, and he says, *"You humans went through all the trouble of making these tunnels and yet rarely send visitors. Don't worry. I'll just follow behind you and do as I please."*

Horokaida rushes to Jean-Pierre's side, opens his medic kit, and takes out a plastic bag of what looks like pale sand. He opens the bag and dumps its contents into the gaping wound in Jean-Pierre's chest. Jean-Pierre shrieks as the sound of flesh burning fills the air, and Horokaida presses his palms together while summoning a strange pressure which emanates out from his body. He touches Jean-Pierre's wound, and it begins to seal itself as Horokaida chants something quietly. Jean-Pierre faints. His breathing slows down.

I ask, "Do you want me to carry him?"

"Nah," Horokaida throws the soldier's body over his shoulders and says, "I've got him. If it gets worse from here, though, I'll have to drop him before I can fight."

"What the hell did that thing say to you?" Ein asks while approaching with a black, double-sided hammer.

"Good Avva," Horokaida exclaims, "is that the weapon they assigned you?"

"Hold on," she retorts with a stern frown. "You can't just ignore my question, Brock, and I wasn't talking to you, Horo."

"Ah, whatever," Horokaida says in a distracted manner and hurries back to his duffel bag to set Jean-Pierre down as he checks the rest of his equipment.

"So, what did it say, Brock? Why did that monster attack Jean-Pierre and just run away?"

"Yeah, dude," Hannibal chimes in with several others as the squad gathers around me, "why did it talk to you and not to one of us?"

"I don't know."

"You're supposed to be a 'veteran,' right?" Hannibal snorts, "Did you say mean words to make it go away or something?"

"No," I tell them. "It's still here. Enrec left behind some lonely monster, and it's decided to tag along—so we'll have to watch each other's backs while moving ahead."

"Brock!" Horokaida yells from where he stands next to his bag, "Check out what weapon they left me with. I lucked out!"

I turn away from the crowd to see Horokaida proudly holding a white sniper rifle in his hands, and now I'm interested in my own present. I go back to my gear while keeping an eye on the others; at the same time, both Horokaida and Ein keep watch over me on instinct.

I open my duffel bag, and, within a large, metallic case, I see that the heaviest piece of equipment is a silver machine gun which looks to be a little bit bigger than an M240. There are a bunch of bullet belts wrapped around the barrel, and they make a clinking sound as I lift the machine gun from the ground.

It's harder to carry than I expected, but I can adjust to its weight. I take one of the ammo belts and wrap it around the top half of my body and leave the others in the ammo pouches that come with the Zega Robe. I drop the spare grenade in the only empty pouch I've got left, next to Alina's bunny, then I rejoin the rest of the group.

"We're already one man down," a skinny, balding, blonde-haired soldier named Magato Ivin says to me while polishing his black-rimmed glasses. "Do you know where that thing will come from next?"

"No. It's playing with us, so we should keep a good distance away from each other."

Horokaida puts his hand on my shoulder and says to Magato with a smile, "Brock's got a lot of experience leading soldiers. So do I, but he looks better doing it."

"How long did you serve?" Magato asks me.

"About seven years. I still know some of the troop leading procedures, but I think that we should improvise for now."

"What do you mean?" Hannibal squints his eyes and tilts his head to the side when he asks me this.

"Ahem," I look at all fourteen squad members as they gather in front of me and explain, "I think that we should advance mostly in line with each other but more spread out than a typical formation would normally be.

"Let's have everyone introduce themselves and what weapons they're bringing to the table."

Horokaida nods and is the first to speak, "I'm Ho—"

"Trade me," Ein interrupts him while pointing at his weapon.

"Huh?" Horokaida all but takes a step back after his thunder's promptly stolen.

"I was a really good sniper back in the day. Trade me."

"Hmph." Horokaida eyes her while stroking his beard with a smirk. "Okay."

He shrugs and hands Ein his sniper rifle; she hands him her hammer. Ein ignores his attempt to introduce himself and introduces herself instead, "My name's Ein Bira, and I'll be watching your backs."

"All right!" Hannibal says, "I'm Hannibal Martin. Shotgun and pistol." He holds up a white, double-barreled shotgun next to a black pistol.

Fichte Evans follows after him: "Sword and pistol," he says with a blade capable of generating flames at his side.

"Magato Ivin," the blond-haired soldier proclaims while raising his own sword and pistol in the air.

"Leon Pyrrho," a freckle-faced man with reddish-blond hair bows to us and indicates the submachine gun in his right hand and a sword that's a little shorter than the others in his left.

"Ha-Joon Ang," a skinny, bearded soldier with long, black hair holds up an Enrec MT Cannon. It's more effective than a machine gun, and the barrel of the weapon is wide enough to fit a lead ball that's hollow in its center; at the center, there's a mix of two different powdered compounds that'll produce a huge explosion upon impact.

"Ashura Ming," a young, bald man with a full beard to compensate for it shows off a short, black spear and raises the assault rifle in his right hand. "Nice to meet everyone," he says.

"Lenaka Ousmane," a buff-looking woman nods to me and reveals a short axe with a black blade and another assault rifle.

"Yafeu Avun…"

"Ife Molovok…"

"Raphael Boucher…"

"Ahiga Nek…"

The rest of our squadmates finish with their introductions, and I take a quick account of everyone's assigned weapons. Yafeu and Ife both have grenade launchers that are less than half the size of the MT Cannon, Raphael's got a long, flaming spear alongside a shotgun, and Ahiga's strapped his assault rifle to his waist in order to take Jean-Pierre's sword and dual-wield two blades. We've got enough soldiers and equipment to put up a solid fight, but we've gotta cover tactics before we go.

"Everyone knows how the jet boots work, right? There's a button inside of the boot and over your big toe. If you raise your feet and press it, you'll take off; to stop, point your feet downward and hit the button again—but don't try it if you're right next to someone or you'll burn them alive."

"Got it," Magato says. "What else? How should we proceed from here?"

"All right, so…" I think it over for a few more seconds, then I know, "Yafeu, Ife, and Ha-Joon are all carrying the most explosive firepower, and that means that they should make up the outermost elements of our formation. Yafeu will take position on the far left and some meters ahead of our more melee-focused units. Ha-Joon only has the ammo to fire his cannon once, so Ife will support him on the rightmost flank of the formation.

"From left to right, it'll be Yafeu, Leon, Magato, Fichte, and Ashura; Horokaida will follow behind them as a team leader. From Ashura, left to right again, it'll be Ahiga, Hannibal, Raphael, Lenaka, Ife, and Ha-Joon; I'll serve as team leader for the right side of our formation. Ein?"

"Yes? What's up?"

"Are you okay with taking on two different roles?"

"I don't want to be the squad leader, if that's what you mean."

"Why not? You'd be perfect for it," Horokaida insists before I can.

"I only came back to Enrec because I've got some personal issues I need to work out. I'll be the best sniper you could ask for, but I don't want to be responsible for everyone else's movements."

"Damn," is my reply as I scratch the back of my head in consternation. "Do we have any Kom Cells that we can use to communicate with each other?"

Magato taps his visor and says, "There's a dial under your chin that you can leave on and use to talk to everyone at the same time,"—he turns the dial and speaks to me through my helmet—"but we shouldn't all talk over each other at once."

"Got it," I say to him. "I guess that means that Horokaida and I will both fill the role of squad leader from here on out. Ein will watch over everyone, Horokaida will lead the charge when it comes to close combat, and I'll provide support to whoever needs it the most.

"We've got the basics down of how our formation will work. All we have to do is stay on line with each other, use the equipment we've got to our advantage as a team, and blast whoever stands in our way. If everyone's ready, let's march."

4
Team Exercise

--

Brock

--

U SING OUR BOOTS TO PROPEL US AS WE GO, we stagger our positions so that our grenadiers are much farther ahead while everyone else is spaced out enough to nearly cover the width of the tunnel itself. Over time, our formation shifts into a diagonal echelon so that the left side moves a little farther ahead than the right; this way, Ha-Joon, the strongest member of our squad, has more protection than anyone else.

We cover a distance of several miles, passing over flat terrain and odd, earth-like mounds pressing through the white-tiled netite. When we've gotten used to moving in rhythm with one another, I hear Onaem's voice speak to me through my helmet: "We've detected a few enemies just up ahead of you. We're going to alter the terrain now to match Alandra's. This is the best training you could ever get, so be thankful, assholes."

The entire tunnel lights up, bright enough to blur my vision, and I hear the sound of cracking earth mixed with metal being warped. Static reverberates throughout the atmosphere, and…

White tiles shift and turn into golden brown plains, where mostly barren hills and uneven terrain await us ahead. The ceiling begins to simulate a blue sky with a hot sun burning overhead, but there's no breeze, not even a sound. Our change of scenery comes with a dry heat that wasn't asked for, but being able to glide compensates for that.

We pass around a series of tall hills that look too identical to be real; behind them, there are several more scattered throughout the rolling wasteland of netite. After crossing over brown, barren earth, we enter a stretch of desert that precedes the lowlands leading up into a vast, dark mountainscape.

Up ahead, a group of tall dunes stand between us and, hopefully, what might be the first camp. Yafeu glides over the first, tallest dune.

A canister buried in the sand explodes at his feet.

White smoke erupts from the canister, and then a bullet strikes Yafeu's helmet. In the same instant, the Zega Suit activates, sending forth a blue charge to protect Yafeu's head and blunt the impact. But, even with the help of the suit, he's knocked straight to the ground—

Right as another canister explodes near Fichte.

Two more erupt with white smoke where Ha-Joon and Ife cross and make our whole formation vulnerable. Yafeu returns to his feet and glides forward with his weapon perfectly intact, but the explosions at the rear have slowed us down.

"Push forward," I announce to everyone through their helmets. "We've got an enemy sniper with his sights set on us already! Outrun the gas and we won't have to stop to worry about whether they're chemical weapons."

"Roger," Horokaida replies.

"Roger," everyone else chimes in.

But, just as we descend from the first ridge, we see a squad of repurposed Alandran drones aiming their rifles up at us. Each one of them has a bright orange marking to indicate their supposed "weak spots." Without waiting another second, I give my orders:

"Yafeu, Ife, and Ha-Joon—don't fire. As for everyone else, shoot and advance!"

Our melee runners keep their distances while those with assault rifles, shotguns, and pistols unload everything they've got upon the drones. I rush to the far right of the formation and then a couple yards ahead so that I'm outflanking our enemies. I drop to the prone position, but, before I shoot, I accidentally hit a small switch on my gun: it causes the sheathe of a metal fist to extend around the barrel of the machine gun and to come together over it. There's still a hole in the middle knuckle of the fist, and so I pull the trigger and hold the butt-stock of the gun tight against my shoulder.

A barrage of heavy rounds explodes from out of the barrel in succession, and, within mere seconds, the entire fist glows red. I tear through an army of maybe twenty drones, then I say to the others, "Ceasefire. Give the fighters some room to work."

On cue, Lenaka leads a charge that's followed closely by Ahiga, Raphael, Leon, and Fichte. They're quickly fired upon by the remaining shooters, but blue sparks fly as lead bullets make contact with Zega barriers and rebound without causing much damage other than the shock of impact. Lenaka cleaves through metallic heads with swift strokes of her axe, and Ahiga dismembers every robotic limb he can see. Fichte ends some of them with a pistol shot to the head and struggles to properly swing his sword, while Raphael plunges into the battlefield with ease, running through each combatant he meets with the same determined glare.

Leon acts more strategically than the rest of the chargers. Rather than taking his targets head-on, he closes the distance between them and sprays at the weak points of three sentinels with his submachine gun before dismantling them all.

I hear the sound of a gun going off in the distance.

A sniper round hits Leon's left boot and pierces it; the boot explodes, and Leon loses his left leg. Blood bursts from his lower body. Leon turns, and I see his guts hanging from his ribcage before he plunges into the sand and turns it red.

"Ein!" I scream, "Get that fucking sniper!"

Magato flies over to Leon's body and swoops down to pick up his submachine gun while tossing the pistol he had. Instinctively, I rush after the pistol and tuck it inside of one of my ammo pouches. "Don't just throw away our equipment," I call after him.

Magato doesn't respond.

The melee team clears out the rest of the drones, and, before I can order everyone to move to Leon's location to protect him, the dunes in front of us are suddenly split down the middle. Colossal wedges of sand break apart and move out of the way of something unnatural.

It looks frozen in place, like a bronze statue. Its body resembles a human's, but it's sculpted with definition that appears stiff and yet constantly moving at the same time. Its eyes, nose, and mouth continually shrink inward, then the figure transforms.

Rivulets of curly, ivory hair flow down and across stone pockmarks that make up a new face, with a narrow slit for a mouth and one big, pupilless eye. Stone facial hair grows to cover its mouth, and its arms and legs enlarge into muscled blocks of stone flesh. The statue looks straight ahead as it bares long, bloody teeth; its expression instantaneously flickers to snarling rage, and it lets out a sound that pierces my eardrums.

It hurts, and it's nothing like any sound made in the real world. This shrill scream echoes out from two separate dimensions, intermingles, and produces a high-pitched ring that sings through the air.

When it moves, its body flashes forward in increments, too quick for me to see. It glares at Ashura, takes one step toward him, and, with the next, thrusts its hand through the center of Ashura's face; it tosses half of it to the side.

Everyone around the monster retreats, and I call over the communication network, "Grenadiers, go!"

But now it's right in front of me.

They don't fire, and it shrieks when I look into the empty, lifeless eye in the middle of its face. Within seconds, the image of the creature starts to shift. I see one dull eye separate into two. Its face becomes clear, sculpted to look humanoid again, but it scowls at me with blood running down from its lower lip.

The statue shoots forward, past my ability to perceive its movements—

I hear the sound of a man's scream mixed with a bat's, and a powerful force strikes below my ribcage. I see the color of white blur before my eyes before zipping away, then I hear the sound of gunshots following behind it.

The strike lands so fast that I've barely time to process it, but I feel sick. I want to move, but it's like a hammer smashed into my lower side, and I'm too stiff to know how bad the damage is. I stay in place for a moment; my vision shakes and blurs, then I hear two more smoke canisters being set off in the distance.

"*You got lucky,*" says the voice of the demon we met earlier in my head, "*the* Ajalu *sensed my presence and was too confused to finish you off. If it had only waited a bit longer, it could've killed us both.*"

I turn off my microphone and manage to utter, "How do we fight that thing?"

Yafeu and Ife begin launching a barrage of black grenades at the demonic statue, but Ha-Joon holds back. The grenades land near the creature, and, just as they detonate, the spirit stalking me says, "*The* Ajalu *are called 'higher-level demons,' but that's only because there is no classification for what they really are. They're beyond your natural perception, Brock. Beyond human perception.*"

Clouds of black smoke rise and fade above the bronze statue, which resembles its original appearance once again.

Ahiga dashes toward the Ajalu and swings at the exact moment its head turns to acknowledge him. Both of their forms seem to intersect before passing one another. A human arm flies up into the air, and Ahiga dashes forward in order to escape as blood spurts from his wound.

"Tourniquet! I need a tourniquet," he shouts over the communication network.

"Ha-Joon," Magato interjects while ignoring Ahiga, "hurry up and blast that thing!"

"No, Ha-Joon," I call over to him. "Wait just a little bit longer."

"Where the fuck have you been, Brock?" Magato shouts, "It's going to kill all of us!"

Just then, a sniper round strikes near Magato's right kneecap. The Zega barrier activates with red static followed by a shower of sparks; the round's impact twists Magato's lower leg out of place before it rebounds into the earth.

Magato begins screaming, and Lenaka, who's gliding next to him, exclaims to everyone, "His barrier's been shut down! Ein, we need a visual on the enemy sniper as soon as possible!"

Ein finally responds, and she does so by shouting over the network: "Run! Something's behind us! Brock, order everyone forward now!"

"What's going on?" Yafeu shouts back.

"What are you talking about," Fichte yells over him.

"Shut the fuck up!" I roar over everyone, "Everyone turn around—"

And there, the greatest devil of them all crawls our way, a devil that pulls the front half of its body forward with two giant, grey hands attached to misshapen arms while a pair of two more arms drags behind it. It has a human head, but it's enlarged out of proportion with the rest of its body, stretching upward and pulling the features of a wrinkled, hollow face into a high mound of molded flesh. Great, pupilless eyes glare back at me like fluid-filled scars of yellow and above a nose that's been sliced in half and a broken jaw which skids across the ground. The grey mass of decaying flesh contorts the more I look at it, and, before I make the next call, Ein says her last words to all of us.

"It doesn't matter what you do! Get the hell out of here! Ge—"

Her transmission cuts off.

"Brock," Hannibal yells, "tell us what to do! Hurry!"

"L-Let's go!" is my response, "Move forward and we can outrun them!"

The rest of my firing squad fires bursts of flames from their propulsion boots, and we surge onward as one united front.

"Someone's dropped a weapon up ahead," Raphael remarks over the network. "Looks like a, uh... heavy machine gun, maybe?"

Raphael soars ahead of Hannibal and Lenaka. He swoops down to grab the handle of the weapon, and it detaches from the chamber below it.

Removing the handle acts as a trigger, and the machine gun explodes, obliterating the lower half of Raphael's body.

When the top half of him hits the ground, Magato cries out, "Look what you did, Brock! You got him killed! Why didn't you stop him?"

Instead of replying, I pay more attention to a dark silhouette seated on a pillar made of rock to the northwest. While Magato continues talking shit to me, I look closer to see the head of a goat affixed to the body of a frail woman. The demon's crossed its legs; two fingers on its right hand point up and the two on its left point down. Just as I start to see the demon clearly, it raises its right hand up higher:

A gigantic face emerges from the ground next to one colossal human hand. The bearded, hollow-eyed face of a titan howls and grabs Ife!

Ahiga, with a tourniquet now sealing off his amputation wound, rushes in and cuts deep into the titan's index and middle fingers. Ife breaks free, and, when Ahiga's sword gets stuck, he draws his assault rifle and fires right into its eyes; at the same time, Yafeu fires a black grenade that almost lands in the titan's mouth.

The goat demon in the distance moves his left hand down, and his pet titan sinks back into the ground as the grenade detonates.

"Ahiga, look out!" I call to him.

He turns to see the bronze, human statue from before, and the two of them confront each other for a brief moment. Ahiga raises his rifle while Ife and Yafeu take aim. They all but pull their triggers at the same time, and two black grenades precede a hail of bullets that smash into the Ajalu's body. Its facial features shrink inward once again, then it rockets forward.

The Ajalu darts straight, toward Ahiga, then it phases through him.

Ahiga's parted right down the middle. He explodes outward as the stone beast crushes his flesh with the strength of its entire body. It passes through the human obstacle in its way and emerges drenched in Ahiga's blood.

The goat demon raises its right hand.

The titan moves from beneath the earth. Ife sees it coming before we do; he fires a grenade, and dust spits out from a crater that opens in the ground. A statuesque hand reaches out from within the crater and grabs both Ife and the grenade before it squeezes tightly.

The grenade detonates with Ife still inside. Blackened flesh spurts out alongside organs between the titan's fingers, and Horokaida screams, "No! Ha-Joon, hurry up and kill it!"

"Negative," I reply while talking over him, "now's not the right time—we have to move ahead!"

Without waiting for a response, I burst forward just as the shrunken-faced statue looms behind me.

Horokaida, Hannibal, Fichte, Magato, Ha-Joon, Lenaka, and Yafeu follow while tightening the formation as we attempt to surge ahead faster than the enemy can keep up with. The ground below us loses all color while the view ahead begins to change into the dim, violet outline of what looks like the ceiling of a cave.

Onaem speaks to us through our communication network:

"Hey, where the fuck are you guys?"

"Modukai Sergeant," I start to explain, "we've taken som—"

"Shut the fuck up! You don't speak to me, you stupid shit-bag! I'm the only one who should *ever* be speaking!

"You've got ten minutes to clear your way to the first camp. After that, we're detonating the fucking tunnel."

Onaem doesn't say anything else, and so Magato starts to speak up, "We're down by seven people! We can't trust you to lead us anymore, Brock."

The ground opens up in front of all of us; the demonic titan reaches forward and grabs for Lenaka; she boosts her acceleration and careens out of the way and at the exact same moment that its entire arm smashes into the ground beside me.

I'm hit with a torrent of wind, but I fly forward in time to see Hannibal and Fichte advancing on my left.

Hannibal triggers a mine, and a current of explosive power skyrockets upward. Both of them dart left and right, respectively, and just before the shockwave of the blast reaches them.

Magato shouts so loudly that it makes my fucking ears ring, "BROCK," the bastard says, "what are we supposed to do? Tell us!"

A black pillar of aura shoots down to the northeast, and the goat demon reappears a good distance ahead of us. To the right, I see it glare our way while gesturing for its pet titan to descend beneath the earth again. To my left...

The tunnel opens up into a vast recess, where small traces of light shines down on an elevated chunk of stone. On top of this landmass, I see the sunken face of a massive, pale green statue. It sits upon a grey throne and watches us with its head tilted to the side.

Fichte looks more transfixed than me. He stares at the statue with so much focus that a sniper round lands near one of his boots and doesn't prompt a reaction.

"Fichte," I call over to him, "what the hell are you doing? Fichte!"

He stops in place, letting the rest of us fly ahead of him before I have to turn around and go back.

"Brock, where the fuck are you going?" Magato screams, "What are—"

"Shut up! I'm not leaving anyone else behind."

Ha-Joon and Hannibal follow my lead, and we both race toward Fichte before the goat devil can trigger its pet. As I'm coming up to him, I see Fichte start to tremble. His head shakes, faster and faster, and then...

It bursts inside of his helmet.

The titan sitting on his throne howls with deep, mocking laughter. Its voice is loud enough to shake the tunnel, and it stops me from thinking straight with a hard, grating tone that won't stop.

"Are you okay?" Ha-Joon asks me, and I nod while gesturing toward the rest of our squad.

"Let's keep going," I tell him. "We have to make it."

"We will," he says. "I'm counting on you."

The two of us regroup with the others, and Magato tries to scold me again, "You can't run off like that if you're going to be leading us!"

"Why didn't you follow me?"

The titan from below breaks through the ground between me and Magato, compelling everyone to dash ahead. While staying on line with one another, Jean-Pierre wakes up and almost pushes Horokaida off balance when he decides to jump off of him.

"Hey," I hear him scream over the network, "what the fuck's going on? Where's everyone else?"

Jean-Pierre looks around in bewilderment, and, at the same time, the burrowing titan disappears underneath the dark earth.

"I need a weapon—somebody help me!" he cries.

"Magato," I call out, "you picked up an extra sword earlier. Give it to Jean-Pierre so that he can protect himse—"

"Wait a minute!" Magato shouts back at me, "Why should I have to give up one of *my* weapons? I want two swords so that I can protect *me*. You obviously aren't going to do that, so—"

"Magato," Horokaida cuts him off, "give Jean-Pierre one of your weapons. It doesn't matter which one."

"I refuse," he says.

"What the hell, Magato?" Hannibal yells over everyone else, "What are you waiting for—give him a fucking sword and let's go!"

Yafeu flies over to Jean-Pierre and gives him his assault rifle. "Thank you," Jean-Pierre says to him, and everyone else turns their attention to another colossal form that towers over us as it walks our way.

From where I'm at, all I can see is a hulking, hunchbacked mass which makes the ground shudder with each step that it takes.

"No," Hannibal mutters out loud, "this isn't right. They're ripping through us like we're nothing—how can this be our training?"

"Be quiet," Lenaka says to him. "Nothing's been normal since we got here, so don't give in to the bullshit now. I—think... you—" her voice becomes distorted as the great giant gets closer.

It covers the distance between us with long strides that I couldn't make out before in the darkness. I know we're at the end of the tunnel—we have to be! All that's standing before us is this hideous sculpture of a creature.

Two human legs, the color of stone, appear below the immense torso of a statuesque man with a melted face. Where its face has been corroded, algae grows out and along its backside. The titan buckles over as he bears the weight of a giant, black-and-white cathedral with white columns surrounding it on one central platform. The cathedral's tall enough to touch the ceiling of the tunnel, and so the titan carries it forward on its back.

It takes its last step toward us, so that it's only a mile away, then it opens jaws filled with splintered teeth and howls. The titan grabs the edges of the foundation, then it throws the whole cathedral at us.

Hannibal screams with a mix of confusion and rage as an object the size of a small town closes in from above. I shoot forward, hoping to race underneath the cathedral—

But it's impossible.

No matter where I go, I won't be safe. Magato and the others begin shouting my name, but I don't know what to say.

"Hurry," is all I can manage to tell them. "Fly as fast as you can!"

While I move north, everyone else darts off in different directions. Their voices compete to be heard as they panic, but they're all saying the same thing: we can't outrun it.

The cathedral and its foundations crash down atop our squad; all that panicked yelling turns to fierce screaming before the building collapses and smashes apart across the ground.

A column falls a few inches away from me, and then a small tower plunges toward my head. I soar to the left, dodge a chunk of brick wall, and move forward to pass under the rest of the debris.

Behind me, the cathedral's broken up into a thick cloud of smoke that shoots out in all directions. From within that storm of smoke and debris, bronze statue-men with shrunken, snarling faces pour out en masse and begin moving toward me in rapid intervals.

Straight ahead, the titanic Ajalu looks down on me without making a move. What's left of its melted face contorts itself into a hateful scowl, like a god beaming rage down upon his subjects.

Lenaka, Yafeu, Magato, Horokaida, and Jean-Pierre emerge from the destruction and stand at my side against the giant Ajalu.

Following them, Ha-Joon appears without his helmet and struggles to catch his breath before he looks to me and says, "Now's the time! Can I use it?"

"Yeah. Go ahead."

Ha-Joon trembles as he sets the Enrec MT Cannon down on a thick tripod and pulls two small levers on its right side. The cannon expands with an outline of netite, of transparent white latticed with neon traces of red. He aims what's now an enlarged mortar at the titan, who takes one great step our way in response. Ha-Joon flexes his arm and uses his hand to push a broad trigger; as he pushes down, radiant energy is steadily generated at the base of the cannon.

As the bronze Ajalu approach in a mob from behind, the stone titan swipes at us with one hand—

Ha-Joon's cannon erupts and produces a blinding light. Enormous power converges at the base of the barrel and explodes outward. The strength of the cannon is so overwhelming that it consumes Ha-Joon's body before creating a blast which soars toward the titan's head.

The blue volley of energy smashes into the Ajalu's skull and shatters it into a million pieces on contact.

The six of us remaining soar on ahead in order to avoid the Ajalu closing in behind us. As the stone giant in front starts to fall over, I can hear everyone gasp almost in unison as we scramble to avoid being crushed by it.

"They've taken so many of us," Magato says quietly. "This can't be real. They couldn't have all died that fast."

"Shut up, Magato," Lenaka scolds him over the network, "there's no poi—"

The ground opens up in front of Lenaka, and the underground titan appears.

She moves just out of its grasp, then it disappears as fast as it emerged. As Lenaka flies over the recess in the ground, it surfaces again, quicker than before, and reaches for Yafeu. Yafeu dodges, but the titan burrows down again and then reappears in front of me!

Stone jaws with pointed teeth open before my eyes, and all I see is a black hole lined with blood right as Horokaida races to my side and pulls me away before the Ajalu can swallow me whole.

Although we increase our speed while plunging farther into the end of the tunnel, the underground titan begins to break up the ground below us. It appears and submerges itself so rapidly now that I'm not sure if I can dodge it anymore.

It appears near me a second time, swings its arm, and slams its open hand down as I narrowly evade being obliterated on the spot. A sniper round strikes an inch away from one of my boots, and that's my cue to keep moving in spite of the Ajalu below us.

Not far in the distance, I see a faint, violet light shining from a door made out of it. A hallway the color of lavender marks the end of the tunnel. On both sides, I notice elevated plateaus that support a series of titanic thrones like the one before.

"We're almost there," I reassure the rest of the team, "this is the home stretch!"

From the very back of the hallway, closest to the door, a giant raises its sculpted hand in the air, and an arm the color of pale green descends as it slices its palm through the air.

Its hand stops, and the ground beneath it becomes a ripple of ruptured earth.

Another hand descends from the opposite aisle: the ground below it crushes inward and bursts out like a wave.

A third and a fourth hand follow, and the entire floor of the tunnel becomes a sea of ravaged earth. The underground titan begins springing out of the ground and disappears amidst the breaking up of the terrain around us.

One of the giants gets up from its throne and stiffly walks over to stand in the center of the hallway.

The pale green statue of a woman looks down on us with a hungry smile and brandishes a sword in one hand. She uses her other arm to hold a child whose face I can't see but whose head is abnormally white. Crawling all over her exposed body are children with warped facial features—eyes pushed to the side of one skull in a column, lips mashed into the eyes or septum of another. One on top of her shoulder glares at us with the face of an enraged adult.

The titan lifts her sword in the air, shrieks, and the other titans swing their arms down again as she slashes downward and sends out a ripple of force which tears apart the ground at our feet.

Jean-Pierre catches some of the impact, and the last thing I see is his left side being ripped from his body. Jean-Pierre dies with his eyes wide open and with a gasp cut short before he can even understand what happened.

The ground sinks in below me, then it springs back up to crash into my knee just as I try to boost myself away from it. I'm thrown upward, and I use my boots to fly back toward level ground—

I overcorrect, and the ground opens up again before I fly into it. The sea of earth takes hold of me.

My vision goes black, and I knock my head against something as dirt and gravel start to cover my body. The ground's broken up into haphazard valleys and crooked ridges, and I'm lying on my face near the bottom of one of those valleys, near a broad rift that leads into the dark abyss below it.

5
Solidarity

--

Brock

--

AT THE BOTTOM OF THE VALLEY, I hear the demon in my head speak to me.

"How do you feel about your performance, Brock? Do you think you did a good job in getting nearly every one of your teammates killed? You're a really stupid human, aren't you, Brock?"

"I don't care about your opinions. You're a demon, and, when you show yourself, I'll end you as soon as you're ready."

"Oh, you still think that you're in control? You're more juvenile than I expected—and I'm more than a demon. I'm an Ukjejido, and that means that I can tell you how this all ends. There's no point in hiding it from you now."

I hear Horokaida call over the radio, "Brock! Where ar—"

His voice cuts off, and no one else reports in.

"The prefrontal cortex is an area in your little human brain where abstract judgments are rendered. It helps with your ability to make logical decisions, and so the frontal cortex projects neurons toward both the prefrontal cortex and the amygdala, where you process fear."

"Brock!" I hear Lenaka call out, but her transmission abruptly cuts off after that.

"When your frail human body experiences stress, it releases epinephrine and norepinephrine as well as glucocorticoids, all in preparation for your 'fight-or-flight' response. Your sympathetic nervous system activates, and the projections leading toward your prefrontal cortex are weakened in favor of connections leading to the amygdala.

"A pruning process can occur from prolonged stress—something you should be familiar with, Brock. Your filthy brain releases LTD and LTP; where LTP strengthens, LTD destroys. Dendritic branches in your hippocampus are destroyed in favor of memories that can be used by the amygdala. You start losing memories that are less relevant. The past becomes foggy, and your 'rational mind' activates true fear learning. This isn't about when or how you kill me, Brock; this is about when and how I get to see you break. Get on your feet, Brock."

I stand and move to pick my machine gun up off the ground. Only half of my helmet remains; the other half has been shredded into nothing. I'm missing one boot, so I take off the other and put it inside my duffel bag before I start walking up the ledge of the valley.

"I'm going to prime you. You won't know until it's all over, but you'll follow what I've said to the letter. Your amygdala will activate the neurons in your basolateral amygdala, activating a desire for fear-based learning. This has all already happened, and that's why you will fail, Brock."

I continue marching up the valley, waiting anxiously for someone else to call out over the radio—even if it has to be Magato.

"You will fail. Your amygdala is much larger than it's supposed to be; your hippocampus has wasted away. I bet that you can hardly remember anything, and you're going to make everyone around you suffer because all your pent-up emotion will block any logic you might pretend to have. Let me tell you exactly how it all goes, okay?"

"Shut the fuck up. Please shut the fuck up and leave me alone."

"She's up there waiting for you. That ugly statue. I'll turn your radio back on, let you hear them die. Your mind's been changed from your contact with the Ajalu. Now you can see what she really looks like."

As soon as the communication network cuts back on, I hear Lenaka's voice cry, "Fire, Yafeu!"

I hear the sound of Yafeu's grenade launcher, and a black grenade lands at the feet of the abomination's new form.

Instead of her statuesque appearance, the female titan from before has become something more menacing. Her body has lost its shape, and, instead of a human woman, a taller being with shriveled, white skin and red slits for its eyes and nostrils hunches over to grab the grenade—

It explodes in the creature's hand, searing through what's left of its forearm before the wretched titan stands tall and shrieks.

Dozens of decrepit giants stand up from their thrones. They unleash a thunderous roar throughout the tunnel and just as Lenaka rushes toward the female titan with her gear still intact. The giant swings wildly, swiping through the air as it moves to obliterate her with one strike.

Lenaka flies up fast enough to burn the titan's arm while hovering above it.

"Lenaka..."

She slashes down with her axe and strikes the shriveled giant in the middle of its forehead, which causes each of the titans to change again.

They reveal themselves as strange, human-like shapes that exist half in reality and half somewhere else, with towering stalks for bodies and sharp spines for legs and arms. Their skulls are like gems stretched into crude, shining faces.

"Lenaka goes first."

Lenaka's axe digs into the tall head of what's now a faceless creature that's missing one arm. It reacts by grabbing Lenaka, and it throws her to the ground.

"Wait!" I hear Yafeu shout while running toward her.

Lenaka gets to her feet, and the abomination stomps her into the earth.

Yafeu screams with rage, launches another grenade—

And I fire my machine gun while trying to outflank the giant.

"Yafeu was so young. It's such a shame."

The grenade explodes, and, this time, it takes one of the titan's lower legs with it. Yafeu prepares another grenade.

"Yafeu, look out!" I yell while spraying the giant bastard with rounds of lead.

The titan falls to one knee, then it raises its arm and brings its fist down upon Yafeu, crushing him into a bloody mess.

Horokaida suddenly rushes into battle, leaps atop the titan's arm, and smashes its head to the side with one powerful blow. The giant falls on its side; as soon as his feet hit the ground, Horokaida makes quick eye contact with me and gestures for me to follow.

"He's not long for this world, either."

As I sprint after him, avoiding the giant before it can re-cover, I hear Horokaida say, "C'mon! We're almost there!"

A diamond-colored titan in front of him swings his arm down, and a wave of pressure causes the earth at our feet to break apart. Horokaida's the closest to the impact. A transparent blast of pressure strikes him at an angle and blows him backward at a rapid speed. Horokaida's body soars into the chaos behind me, and, just as I see the giant raising its fucking hand again, I bolt forward, into the violet portal ahead...

The noise behind me begins to fade, and the way beyond turns completely uniform. I enter a deep purple haze, and soon I can only hear the sound of my footsteps before the tunnel's true appearance returns.

Now that I'm beyond the simulation, white netite stretches in front of me within a long hallway shadowed with white mist.

"Recruit," I hear Onaem speak over the radio, "you've got three fucking minutes before we blow up the whole tunnel. Your squad ended up with what we call a 'bad lane,' so we showed a little extra patience once we saw the casualties getting worse. You need to get the hell out of there before you compromise the safety of the entire base—hurry the fuck up!"

Magato flies into me. As I'm tackled from the side, he punches me in the face as he tries to climb on top of me.

I kick him in the stomach and then push him off with another kick to the chest. Magato falls on his back but quickly rolls over, draws his pistol as he rushes to stand, and aims the barrel at my face.

"You're no leader! You failed everyone who put their trust in you—you got them all killed, you stupid bastard!"

"Magato, wait—"

"This is all your fault. You should've let *me* lead us—ugh! Why did we give you any authority? I'm going to put you down for what you did to us!"

A sniper round pierces the side of Magato's head and knocks him to the ground. I move toward my machine gun while keeping my eyes ahead, and the small silhouette of a stranger holds up one hand while approaching in the distance.

I drop my guard, and he lowers his rifle to one side; with one free hand, he draws a pistol and aims it at my head.

"That's right," he says while beaming a grin at me. "You're the last one."

A blond-haired man with a high-and-tight haircut and a black jumpsuit steps to the side and then gestures ahead with his pistol. "Drop the big gun and walk ahead of me. And take off that stupid helmet."

I let my weapon drop to the ground, throw away what's left of my helmet, and proceed forward.

"That was easier than I expected. I was hoping for a bigger fight."

"I failed."

"What was that?" he asks while raising his gun so that it's next to his ear.

"I fucked up."

"Nah. You didn't fuck up. I saw how you handled yourself out there, and you kept your cool through to the end. Respect, brother. What's your name?"

"Brock."

"Just 'Brock?' No last name?"

"Nah. I gave up on the idea of that after my daughter passed."

"I'm sorry to hear that, Brock. Now get on your knees and put your hands behind your head. I promise it'll be painless."

"Thank you."

"'Thank you?' That's all? No last prayer or anything?"

"Someone stopped me from doing what you're about to do years ago, and I always hated him for it."

"You shouldn't," he says. "You'll be a great commandant one day."

"What?"

"Stand up, Brock. I was just joking."

Again, I do as the man says.

"Turn around."

I'm met with cold, grey eyes that study me before we shake hands.

"Brock, my name is Commandant Zeno. I'm one of eight of the Alandran Brigadier Generals, and I am your enemy. Let's keep walking," he gestures ahead while I follow at his side. "They'll blow this place to hell in a few seconds, and the 'camp' you're headed to is just beyond this door. There's a device at the 'camp' which can teleport people in and out, and that's where I was planning on going after I shot you in the face. But, Brock, your face isn't hard on the eyes, so I don't mind talking with you for a moment."

He opens the door to a black chamber with white, latticed patterns running through what looks like a room in the shape of a black oval. The flooring looks like black, jagged marble that's concave at the bottom. Next to a row of human-sized capsules with bright blue glass, there's a grey door panel in the shape of an octagon. Other than that, there is no "camp." Just a vast, hollow space which echoes with Commandant Zeno's voice as he continues speaking:

"Alandra is the better country, and you just don't know it yet. I feel sorry for you," he says as we stride down a dark ledge, "you've been fighting for an illusion."

"I gave up my time for this country. It's not an illusion."

The Commandant glances back at me and replies, "I respect you for your service. It's not for ordinary soldiers to understand where they fit into the bigger picture. You have your cause, and I have mine; there's no room for bitterness here."

"Why is your country so much better then, huh?"

"It raised me well," he replies. "Made me a whole person and made me see my city as a nation of people whose lives are valued more than you could ever know."

Commandant Zeno steps near the capsule on the far left, turns to me, and says, "Brock, I want you to join the Alandran military. I won't take 'no' for an answer, and, in the end, you won't either."

"What do you mean? You th—"

Zeno cuts me off with his laughter. "You're on a doomed journey, soldier. It's not going to get easier, and it's not going to make sense, either. Your chain of command is going to come back, tell you that you're a failure, and then they'll send you out again to die unprepared. There are worse demons in these tunnels than that wretched one sitting on your back," he says while looking over my head with a scowl. "Alandra made sure that you had no way forward. You won't make it to the next camp."

As soon as he steps within the open frame of the capsule, tiny blue particles surround his body to form a floating vat. The vat starts to dissolve his figure, and Zeno says to me, "They'll come back, then they'll fuck you up. If you make it through this, join Alandra."

The capsule spits out blue particles in rapid bursts as the Commandant's body becomes a grey silhouette before being dissipated as it vanishes out of sight.

As if on cue, I hear Onaem's voice screaming from a speaker overhead, "Hey motherfucker, how about you press the red fucking symbols on the capsules' side panels already! Why the fuck did you take so long to make it here—hurry up!"

I do as he asks, tapping on the red hourglass symbol common to each of the panels. Seconds pass, then they all alight in sequence; three bodies phase into existence within each one, and Onaem immediately steps out to stare at me with a bewildered expression.

"You've gotta be fucking kidding me," he says. "You can't be the only one."

"Oh Avva!" shouts Modai Sergeant Kusinon as he steps closer to me and points his finger an inch away from my nose, "You got them all killed, didn't you? What,"—Kusinon jabs me in the face—"did you kill them? Did you?"

Kusinon punches me again, but I don't show him any emotion. He pulls me close while Sergeant Onaem and Sergeant Vladik scream into both of my ears: "You fucking loser! You got them all killed—get on the ground!"

All three of them shove me to the ground at once. As a fourth Sergeant begins to phase in, Onaem screams, "Do pushups, killer! It's your fault! It's all your fault, so you're going to work out as hard as all fifteen of them would've if you hadn't fucked up, all right? All right, you little shithead," he whispers in my ear while getting down on one knee, "I knew you'd fuck this up from the start. No one else lost as many people as you did—that's why we're all here! We were ordered to come babysit you while they send reinforcements, and we don't HAVE the manpower for reinforcements!"

Onaem punches me in the head and walks away. He screams, "Fucking Avva," and kicks the ground.

The guy who just phased in, Modai Sergeant Bach, runs over to Onaem and asks, "What the fuck's going on? Where's the rest of his squad?"

"Go over there and kick him in the stomach before I do— he's a fucking idiot!"

"Roger," Sergeant Bach hurries over to me and does just that; he drives one white boot into my stomach, and I fall to the ground.

Two of them grab onto my uniform and pull me back up while screaming, "Keep pushing! Take off your duffel bag, moron!"

When I try to do this, I'm kicked again before I can get the bag off my back.

"Stand up!" Onaem screams with enough force to spit in my face.

I stand to my feet, he points at my bag, and he says, "Empty it out! Where's your fucking weapon, soldier?"

"I los—"

Onaem punches me again and replies, "Wrong answer! Empty your bag and let us see what made it with you—and where's your boots?"

When I don't respond, Kusinon punches me this time and repeats, "Empty your fucking bag!"

Again, I do as they say without any complaints. As I allow the contents of my bag to spill out, I hear Onaem say to

Kusinon, "He took those punches pretty well, didn't he? He's a strong idiot."

"That's right," Kusinon adds, "strong and useless. He lost everybody."

Sergeant Bach brushes aside my medic's kit and stoops down to pick up a small, black square. He holds it up and looks me in my eyes as he says, "You see this, soldier? This piece connects to fourteen others, and you lost all fourteen of them by letting your squadmates die."

Bach sneers and continues, "It's the best fucking weapon we have—you were supposed to bring every piece back with you, and you fucked that up, too! Get down. Start pushing before we all beat the shit out of you. Get down!"

I do as he says, then all four of them surround me and curse my name.

"Brock," Onaem addresses me, "that's the name of this recruit. We lost all those people because we chose a guy named 'Brock' to be in charge."

"Pfft," Kusinon utters, "who made that decision?"

Kusinon kicks me in the stomach, causing me to gasp for air and clutch at my side.

"C'mon, keep going, fucker!" Onaem shouts as he kicks me, "Don't stop until you bring them all back from the dead. You owe us that!"

"He's right," Vladik chimes in, "you owe us, soldier—push faster!"

Vladik kicks me in my right side, and my arms give. I fall while in the midst of louder screaming. I feel the impact of another kick, but it doesn't hurt. One of them hits me in the back of the head, but I no longer feel pain. All I feel is hot fire running down the back of my neck.

They kick and punch me, curse me for how much I've let them down, order me to keep pushing…

And I hear its voice.

"It's me again. I told you that you would fail, and you thought that you could fight your fate. You can't keep going. I can feel how tired your

body is, Brock. How do you feel, Brock? Do you feel like you're ready to fail again? Again and again?" It laughs, drowning out the shouting from above me, and it says, *"Oh yes, I can put you through much more stress. You have muscle cramps all over now. Your heart's bound to give out before you do. While your bones begin to break, let's go back, shall we? Let's go far back into your memories—let's see what made Brock 'Brock,' shall we?*

"Oh, this looks like a good one. Who's 'Kalina?' Oh, I see. Your humankin. What ugly worms they ar—"

"Shut up!" I scream out loud.

The four Sergeants above me are briefly startled into silence, then they begin shouting again:

"What the fuck was that?" screams one.

"Did he just yell back at us? I know he didn't just yell back at us!" shouts another as he kicks me in the stomach.

All at once, each capsule lights up to summon in four more soldiers with duffel bags on their backs and an assault rifle strapped to the side of each one.

"Get over here," Onaem shouts, and a broad-chested, black-haired soldier leads the way as a bald, chubbier guy follows with two women behind him.

As they form a rank in front of Onaem, two more soldiers arrive and fall in to two separate columns on the right of the formation. When each capsule stays silent from then on, we're left with seven recruits, including me.

"Hold on, guys," Onaem says and raises his hand. "We've got the only survivor from the last run. Everyone else died because of this scumbag. Everybody, meet Brock, the lowest member of this squad. Because of Brock, you're all going to run as fast as you can around the perimeter until we tell you to stop. If you drop your duffel bag or slow down at all, I, Sergeant Bach, or Sergeant Kusinon will be there to correct you. You don't want to find out what that means."

On cue, Bach screams, "Go! Get fucking moving right now! Fucking GO!"

Most of them hesitate before running off in a huff. One or two glances back in confusion, then they curse as they struggle to begin running with all that weight on their backs.

Sergeant Vladik sees to me personally. "Start doing squats in fronts of me," he says.

My body shakes as I get to my feet; in the background, I hear the other Sergeants screaming; the demon in my head says, "*He reminds you of someone, doesn't he? Someone who you don't want to think about.*"

I position my feet in line with my shoulders, and, before I start, Vladik says to me, "Hmm. Looks like you're in good shape. Go ahead, I won't be mean to you. You could use a break, even if you are a murderer."

"I'm... I'm not a murderer. I didn't kill them."

"What was that?" Vladik steps toward me with one hand raised to his ear and says, "Did I tell you to say anything?"

"*Oh yes,*" chimes the demon, "*there it is. When you were younger. Another man...*"

"You know what I'd do with you if they weren't around?" he whispers in my ear, "I bet you'd like it. Keep going."

"*An older man followed you into a room. He locked the door behind him, then he looked at you. What did you see?*"

"*Shut up,*" I finally manage to say back to him. In my anger, I forget about my exhaustion. "*Nothing happened to me. Nothing happened to me.*"

"*Oh, but it did. I see what he did. I know what he did.*"

Sergeant Vladik kicks in the back of my knee and pushes me to the ground. He grabs my neck and says, "I want you to do pushups again. I want to see how good your form is."

"*A group of men tried to undress you once. What happened there, Brock? Did you want to hurt all those people? You broke someone's jaw and gave someone else a concussion, and that's not even the half of it. You should've just let them do it.*"

"No," I mutter out loud.

Vladik smacks me in the back of the head. "What did you say? You got all those good soldiers killed, remember? That was because of *you*, because *you* let them die. You're fucking pathetic, and I'll do you right here—in front of everyone. I'll let them see what a weak-minded individual you are. Push! Push!"

"You're moving away from that memory, and now you're drawn toward another, I see. We're back to 'her' again. That pitiful human you made your wife. How does it feel to know that the woman you loved put a gun to your head?"

"Stop," I warn him.

"What was that?" Vladik screams.

Vladik kicks me, but I don't feel it this time.

"Oh, that's funny. She thought you were 'cheating.' She thought that you were a nuisance—how dare you even think of leaving her! I love watching her hit you."

"Stop it."

"She pointed the gun at your daughter, said she looked too much like you, like a nuisance."

"Stop it! Shut up!" I stand to my feet and clench my fists.

Vladik punches me in the back of the head, screams something that I can't hear, and the demon continues its abuse.

"When you stopped her, she shot you. She saw you as trash. She saw her as tras—"

Vladik grabs my shoulder, then he touches the stuffed animal tucked into one of my ammo pouches and says, "Why the fuck do you have this, recruit? This is trash you don't need!"

I turn around and elbow him in the face.

"She wasn't trash," I say out loud.

Sergeant Vladik falls to the ground unconscious.

"She'll never be trash. Don't ever say that again."

"Ha! Look at what you've done," it taunts me. "They'll kill you now! They're bound to kill you—this was too easy!"

I hear Onaem's voice screaming at me in the distance. All three sergeants move toward me, all three shouting at the tops of their lungs, and then…

Two people descend from the dark cliffs above us. One of them is a man who limps forward while dragging a hammer covered in blood and soot along the ground; on his back, the top of his duffel bag has been torn open, with his medical kit and gas mask close to tumbling out onto the ground.

Behind him, a woman carrying a sniper rifle puts her hand on his exposed arm and asks if he's all right. Horokaida nods to Ein, and the two survivors head in my direction while everyone else stops to look.

"No fucking way," Onaem mutters while staring at them in awe.

Just when Sergeant Kusinon reaches me, he turns toward them and asks the other sergeants, "How did they survive the blast? Have they been back there this whole time?"

As Vladik regains consciousness, Sergeant Bach helps him get to his feet. "What happened?" Vladik asks, but Bach ignores him and just points at them instead, whispering, "More survivors. They weren't supposed to make it."

Onaem's the first to approach them. He walks up to Horokaida, extends his hand expectantly, and says, "Give me your bag."

Horokaida obeys, and Onaem hurriedly dumps out its contents. Sergeant Kusinon rushes to his side and picks up one of the black, square pieces that they gave me such a hard time over. "He's got it," he says while making eye contact with everyone else.

Onaem points at Ein and asks, "Where's your bag?"

"I couldn't bring it with me," Ein replies while looking down in shame.

"Why not?"

"I was separated from it."

"You mean you lost it."

"Yes, Sergeant."

Onaem walks up to Ein and slaps her. Horokaida grabs Onaem's wrist, shouts, "Hey," and Kusinon promptly punches Horokaida in the face. Vladik, having already forgotten about me, walks over to them with Bach; Bach and Vladik kick in the backs of their knees and push them to the ground. Onaem calls out to the rest of the recruits, "Everybody get the fuck over here right now!"

As they all gather into formation in front of me, Onaem gestures for me to join them. "Go ahead," he says. "I'm not mad at you anymore."

As I fall in line, all four sergeants scream for them to start pushing. Ein manages to obey for a short time, but her body quickly gives out. Ein falls when her arms can't take it anymore, and Vladik kicks her.

I react by stepping out of formation so that I can stop them, but Onaem quickly points his assault rifle at my head and says, "Don't do it. Another step and I'll blow your head off. You're lucky they even survived." He gestures at the others with his weapon and says, "Get back in formation before I blow your brains out in front of them."

When I do as he says, the black-haired recruit who's built like a tank grabs my arm and scolds me, "Don't do it again, loser. That's why you got everyone killed. You're an idiot."

I brush him off and continue without commenting. Behind me, I hear him utter "idiot" once again.

As Ein struggles to get her strength back, Vladik grabs the back of her head to start whispering obscenities I can't hear. Horokaida tenses up and begins pushing faster. "Let her go," he warns Vladik. "She fought harder than any of us."

What he says riles them all up, and so Vladik and Bach re-focus their aggression. "Okay then," Vladik replies while forcing Horokaida to his feet. Vladik and Bach restrain Horokaida's arms behind him; Kusinon kicks him in the stomach. Horokaida coughs up blood, and Onaem speaks over him:

"If she can't handle a basic exercise, then she's wasting our time by being here!"

Onaem punches him in the stomach, but Horokaida only grunts and looks down. Onaem smirks, then he looks back at our formation as he lectures us.

"So, we ended up with three survivors. Three survivors out of fifteen good men. We lost twelve people, everyone, and it's because three fucking losers couldn't keep their shit together enough to help out their fellow soldiers. These three are a disgrace to our unit—they'll get you all killed if we take them with us to Alandra without proper discipline,"—Onaem aims his assault rifle at Ein's head while Kusinon kicks her sniper rifle away from her—"and so we're going to give Horokaida here a choice. His friend lost all of her gear, which means that we're going to kill her for failing to be accountable for her equipment.

"We can either do this, Horokaida, or we'll keep pushing both of you until you two die from dehydration. What'll it be," Onaem raises his voice while getting in Horokaida's face, "let us kill her or work yourself to death? Which one? Hurry up!"

Horokaida hesitates, fixes his eyes to the ground, and then he looks back up without showing any clear expression.

"She didn't do anything wrong," he says. "If you want to shoot someone, shoot me. She gave me her gear to protect me, so I'm the one who should be punished."

Onaem strikes Horokaida in the head with his rifle, knocks him to the ground, and shouts, "That's a fucking lie and you know it!"

"I didn't give him my equipment," Ein interjects. "I lost my gear. I'm responsible for not bringing it, so shoot me."

"Oh, we're gonna shoot *both* of you," Onaem replies and proceeds to kick Horokaida in his side. "Push," he screams, "go until you die! If you give up, then I'll shoot!"

Ein and Horokaida begin again, now drenched in sweat and devoid of any emotions. Ein begins pushing right next to her comrade, and all four sergeants condemn them in unison. When they fail to complete a rep, they hit them. They hit them again and again, then Onaem yells at our formation: "Tell them what they are! Tell them what they are—that they're failures, that they lack discipline, that they don't belong here!"

While everyone else joins in on cursing Horokaida and Ein, I hear the demon in my head whisper to me, "*Why don't you join, too? Those sergeants spared your life, so you should be grateful. If they tell you to hate them, then you should hate them.*"

In my mind, I say back, "*I don't hate them. This isn't right.*"

"*How do you know? Maybe they held back. Maybe they're really the ones responsible for your failure.*"

I step out of formation and speak out loud, "No one's responsible for my failures but me."

Another recruit exclaims, "What? Shut up, loser." When I step past him, he gets loud enough to alert the other recruits as he asks, "Hey, what are you doing? Get back here!"

I stride toward Horokaida and Ein, and a skinny soldier with spiked, red hair grabs my shoulder.

"Get back in formation, asshole! Have you lost your mind?"

I brush his hand off and begin walking faster. At my back, the whole formation erupts in anger, calls me an "idiot," a "buddy-fucker."

When I get to the sergeants, Bach tries to grab me, too, but I step past him with even more aggression and move to stand by Horokaida. All four sergeants aim their rifles at me and scream so loudly that it's easy to block them out. In the midst of their shouting, the demon tries to add his input, but I block him out as well.

I get down, then I start pushing with them. They're still screaming, but I use my adrenaline to work just as hard as Horokaida and Ein. I feel them kick me and punch me in the head, but I don't give them any satisfaction. I grunt through pain that no longer matters.

Horokaida smiles at me, and I smile back at him.

"Do you wanna know how I survived?" he asks.

I nod in response while in the middle of another rep.

Horokaida looks ahead and says, "Just clear your mind. I'm going to show you what zol feels like. That's how I keep going."

Within a couple of seconds, I notice that the fatigue I felt before starts to drain away. Although I'm still pushing my body, I feel the pain less and less. Whenever I'm struck, their blows feel negligible. For the first time, I can sense energy radiating out from Horokaida's body; Ein appears to sense it, too. Together, the three of us fight through exhaustion and continue pushing until the sergeants begin backing away.

Onaem pauses while Kusinon whispers something to him. In response, he says to Kusinon, "I don't know. I don't understand it, either."

"Why aren't you tired?" Vladik asks us.

"Because we're not going to give up," Horokaida bellows.

Horokaida descends, and, when he pushes himself back up, he shouts again, "We're not going to give up!"

In unison, the three of us do the same. Each time, we repeat the same phrase, and I feel bolder the longer we hold out.

At last, Onaem tells us all to "Shut up," then he looks back at the formation and says to them, "What are you all waiting for? Your comrades are over here giving it everything they've got! Push with them! Hurry up!"

All four sergeants aim their weapons at the formation, coercing them to join in on our struggle. As the red-haired recruit from before takes his place at my side, he glares my way, saying, "Good going, moron, you got us all fucked up."

"I don't care," I tell him. "These people are my friends. They had my back, so I'll fight for them."

He goes quiet, and Horokaida smiles at me again.

"That's the spirit," he says. "I'm going to show you how to get stronger, Brock. We're all going to get a lot stronger, and we'll make it through whatever lies ahead."

6
Private Ronas

--

Brock

--

"*H*E REMINDS YOU OF SOMEONE, *doesn't he?*"

"Don't bring it up."

"*Private Ronas. Do you remember him?*"

"He's gone now. It doesn't matter anymore."

"*Then why does your amygdala light up every time I pass over his name, every time you see Horokaida. Horokaida reminds you of him. Why?*"

--

Eight years ago, my country set up an outpost down in Gaspul. At F.O.B. Inath, I met Private Ronas.

Eight years ago, Private Ronas and I served in the same battalion, the same company. We trained together as a team. I was the heavy machine gunner; he was the ammo bearer. When Ronas got stronger than me, we switched roles. I carried his ammo in the field and watched his back; he charged ahead and showered our enemies with suppressive fire. We supported a squad of fourteen other soldiers, and our company was one of the first in our battalion to clear a path through the southern districts of Gaspul.

Eight years ago, all those years ago…

Dammit.

I was at F.O.B. Inath again. I walked into a room, and there he was.

Twelve soldiers surrounded him. Private Ronas was bent over a pair of wooden crates, his trousers and underwear pulled down to his ankles. Twelve soldiers took turns on him, and one said to me, "He deserves it." He told me that Ronas had beaten another soldier, that he'd raped this soldier along with his wife and kid.

The twelve of them demanded that I join, and I refused. I walked up to Ronas instead; I tried to get his attention. I wanted him to stand up and fight them with me. Together, we could've stopped all of them.

I asked him to stand, and Ronas looked back. He said, "I'll kill you."

I asked him why, and he responded, "Because I hate you, too. You'll all die. I'll make sure of it."

I tried to fight for him, and they beat me down. Two soldiers held me back as the others kept violating him. Ronas went silent; on the inside, I screamed.

--

"*You let him get raped.*"

"No. I ran out of the room to find help! I found a Modai Sergeant, told him about what happened, and he dismissed me."

"*You didn't help him.*"

"I *did* help him."

"*You were too weak. You let him down. What happened to Private Ronas, Brock? Tell me what happened to your best friend.*"

--

On the battlefield, in the Gizijani District, we almost lost our whole company. Enemy mortar teams blasted through our positions across the open desert terrain; they blew up Private Irikson, Modukai Sergeant Porteg, Modai Sergeant Buva, and several others. We ran across improvised explosives laid in traps set by the enemy, and squads of Gaspulan fighters opened fire on those of us who survived the first barrage of attacks.

Ronas and I retreated West and into a series of shallow trenches dug within rows of tall sand dunes. Behind us, two soldiers went down; one of them was beyond help, and the other had lost a leg. I went back to try to carry her with us, but her heart stopped along the route to escape. Her name was Private Esca, and I started giving her chest compressions in order to resuscitate her heart.

Ronas shot her in the head.

When I stood to confront him while drenched in blood, sweat, and sand, he aimed his rifle at my face and smirked.

"I used to think that *they* were the enemy," he said. "I thought that *we* were the heroes.

"But heroes don't go and rape each other, do they? I bet you did it to me, too, Brock. You were with them, and you didn't stop them from doing what they did, so you must've done it, right?"

"No! I tried—"

"Shut up," he said and glanced away briefly before looking back at me. "There are no more heroes. I'm going to kill you now, and I want you to remember what I said before you die."

He pulled the trigger.

Nothing.

Ronas ran out of ammo. I walked toward him...

--

"That's not all. Why don't you tell me the rest?"

"That's all I need to say."

"And yet I can feel it creeping through your mind, Brock. It's a thought which you don't wish to keep, but you can't escape it. Don't try to grab your stuffed animal for comfort; Alina can't save you now. I know what you did. Say it."

"I protected myself."

"That wasn't you, was it? Ronas pulled the trigger, you walked toward him, and..."

"I hit him with my rifle. I hit him too hard. That's what you want me to say."

"You cracked his skull. You murdered him."

"No! He was my friend. I didn't—I didn't want to—"

"You killed Ronas, Brock. You hit him so hard that your unit took home another dead body. They asked you to read out a eulogy that you'd written, and you lied.

"You said that the enemy killed him. You lied."

"I didn't lie! He tried to—"

"You should've let him reload and finish the job. You didn't protect him. You killed Ronas, and you lied about it. You're a murderer. Just like you did before, all those men are dead because of you. Those Sergeants

are right: you're a failure. You'll do it again. You'll fail, and everyone will die because of you."

"I won't fail! I can make it."

"You got her killed, too—"

"Shut up!"

"You should've been a better father—"

"Shut the hell up!"

"While you struggle, the whole world sinks around you. Poor Alina. She deserved bett—"

"NO! No more! Shut up! Shut up! Shut—"

7
Room Clearing

--

Brock

--

I REACH FOR ALINA'S BUNNY AND GRAB IT TIGHT. While in formation, I break out into a cold sweat. Its voice is gone.

Nine of us stand in a room glowing with blue netite. Before us is a pale blue door, and all four sergeants wait at our side as Onaem starts to explain what's about to happen.

"Everyone, beyond the first camp is a series of chambers connected to one another. There are at least fifty of these chambers, each built with the intent of simulating how we'll expect you to traverse various buildings within Alandra. Originally, this section was just like the area you already passed through: one big tunnel. Enrec found it more convenient to split this tunnel into multiple rooms, which has helped us shrink the presence of both demons and the Ajalu spawn down into individual sectors.

"Rather than have you charge in across open terrain like before, these netite chambers were built so that soldiers could conserve their energy and focus on the tactics used in close-quarters combat while moving forward. Sergeant Kusinon,"—Onaem extends his hand—"hand me your duffel."

Kusinon carries his bag with both hands and carefully hands it over to Onaem, who grunts while taking out a short, black pillar surrounded in a circle by what looks like small, blue diamonds. Onaem's face reddens as he gently lowers the object and sets it upright on the ground, then he gestures to all of us and says, "Everybody needs to take out their black chips and hand them over. They should all have the exact same markings; if they don't, we're fucked. Hurry up," he orders solemnly.

Once we've done as ordered, we reform as Onaem begins laying each piece down on a separate diamond. He adds a few more of his own, and, in total, fifteen black squares marked with red "x's" are set in place and emit a pale ruby light.

"Good, good," he mutters while nodding to himself. Onaem looks up at us and continues, "I said before that most of our squads had made it to their first camping locations. I lied.

"Recruits, we lost ten squads during the first training exercise. That's over a hundred men. We didn't know that our tunnels leading into Alandran territory were as polluted as we understand them to be now, and, for that, I'm sorry.

"Ahem," Onaem straightens up and goes on without showing a hint of emotion, "but that's the nature of war, and you all know it. We didn't expect it, but it happened, and now we have to make adjustments. What you need to understand is that there's no going back for us." He gestures his thumb at the door and says, "We have to cross through fifty chambers and make it to the next camp. From there, we'll be getting picked up in transit to rendezvous with the rest of the reconnaissance forces above ground. Sergeant Bach, go ahead and show them how we'll begin clearing each room as we proceed."

"Roger," Bach nods his head and promptly takes a series of small, black spheres out of his bag.

He stands each one up upon a set of three dark prongs; a green halo comes alight at the top of each dome, and black panels slide away from screens flickering with particles of blue light.

"These are the drones you'll be using as you progress through this next section. We've only got a limited supply, and the six you see here are all that have been made available to us. They serve two purposes: surveillance and destruction. If you see something that's too risky to engage, blow it up."

Sergeant Vladik begins passing out what looks like tiny controllers with clear, glass screens. As he does, Onaem calls out the names of the six soldiers who'll be making use of them:

"Stegan, Dong-Sun, Aro, Tyrick, Syra, and Angoli are all the ones we've deemed responsible enough to handle this equipment. The three losers we have with us have already lost some of their gear, so we're trying things out again with a new batch. If you all fuck it up this time, though, that'll be it.

Sergeant Bach and my colleagues can walk you through the basics, but protocol calls for at least three drones per chambers of this particular size. Sergeant Bach, go ahead and explain—my throat's getting dry."

As Bach continues in Onaem's place, Sergeant Onaem strides over to the machine which contains all fifteen black squares and crouches down next to it while pulling up a holographic keyboard. At the same time, he grabs what looks like a beer from one of his ammo pouches and quickly downs the whole thing.

Sergeant Bach elaborates, "Brock was the leader of the last training exercise, and he ruined it. So, after we've sent in our scouting units, Brock will be the first one to pass through that door. All of you will line up in a very specific order outside of it, with the three failures being the first three to go in—"

"Wait a minute," Vladik interjects while placing his hand on Ein's shoulder; as she twitches uncomfortably, he says, "This one's a sniper, so I think we should place her toward the rear,"—Vladik points to Horokaida and says—"He's our second biggest guy, next to Dong-Sun. We should move him to the middle of the formation, where he can hold things down if they get too rough."

"Very well," Bach replies with a nod and then points at me. "Get the fuck over there, next to the door. Dong-Sun, Stegan, and Tyrick should follow behind you."

Sergeant Kusinon starts to give me his assault rifle, then he pauses to stare at me for a moment before changing his mind. He hands me the pistol out of his pouch instead and tosses me a broad knife. "You don't deserve it," he tells me. "I hope they blast you as soon as you run in."

I don't make any effort to reply, so Kusinon grabs my shoulder and shouts, "Say, 'Yes Sergeant,' asshole!" I tell him what he wants to hear, then I take my place outside of the metal door. Dong-Sun, the black-haired soldier who's a few heads taller than all of us, moves to stand behind me while muttering something under his breath. Stegan and Tyrick angrily side-eye me as they get behind him.

Kusinon strides up to the door, inputs something on a clear, digital pad, and we hear the lock mechanism within spring open.

"Everyone here should already know the drill. The first man in will turn to the right and move to clear the east sector; the second will turn to the clear the west; numbers three and four will follow the same pattern, and we'll form a staggered rank that pushes forward once we know that we're all good to go.

"Before anyone goes charging in, though, let's go ahead and make use of the surveillance drones. From each of your keypads, you should be able to see whatever the drones see; you have miniature cameras in your hands with infrared vision. Even if something invisible's moving around in there, you're gonna notice it because these things pick up heat signatures.

"Dong-Sun, I'm going to open the door just enough for three drones to slide through, and then I'll lock it back in place. Copy?"

"Yes Sergeant," Dong-Sun nods while setting his drone on the ground.

Dong-Sun manipulates his keypad to stimulate flight. His surveillance drone spits out small, grey spindles along the mid-section of its body, and these spindles rotate at a speed so rapid that the drone falls on its side. Kusinon quickly steps in, whispers, "Idiots," and picks the thing up from the bottom before throwing it into the air. The drone wobbles before hovering in equilibrium, and Kusinon shouts, "Hurry up and send them in! Stegan, Tyrick, go!"

They follow his instructions and send two drones behind a leader which creeps beyond the door. Once they've passed this barrier, Kusinon quickly shuts and locks the entrance to the next room back in place. All at once, those of us without a view gather around those holding portable cameras.

"Shouldn't they be standing back?" Vladik asks.

But Bach and Kusinon both brush off his comment, "It doesn't matter," Bach says. "Everyone needs to see what we're gonna be dealing with. They need to know."

When I try to get a look at Dong-Sun's camera, he flinches and backs away, but Kusinon yells at him, "Chill out. Even if he's a loser, we still need him."

I look through the lens, and Kusinon touches a button which turns a clear image of cold, white space into an infrared view of the open chamber. When Dong-Sun looks straight ahead, toward a red door, nothing appears to be in the immediate vicinity. The camera issues a playback recording of what sounds like light, muffled breathing.

In the right corner of the room, I spot a shape that burns red at its center and orange from its outline.

"Look!"—Tyrick points—"Are those... horns?"

Sure enough, two slender spikes stick up from an elongated head. I see what looks like glowing red fur from a shape seated toward the very back of the room. The longer I look, the more it seems like flames of red and orange expand and swirl around its figure. I feel lightheaded, nauseous.

"Turn it off," I tell them.

"Excuse me?" Sergeant Kusinon shouts and aims his rifle at my face. "Did someone tell you to fucking say someth—"

"He's right!" Tyrick exclaims, "That thing's not normal! Turn it off!"

Sergeant Vladik pushes Tyrick and shouts, "Shut the fuck up!"

"Change views," Kusinon orders Dong-Sun, "take off the infrared so we can see what it actually looks like."

Dong-Sun doesn't hesitate. He touches the screen, removes the red glare, and grey fur emerges in its place. I see the body of a human below the long, horned head of a goat. Two fingers point skyward on one hand; the other two point toward the ground on the other.

Tyrick screams. He drops his drone on the floor while reaching to tear at the hair on his head. I look into the black, beady eyes of the Ajalu, and I realize that it's the same one from earlier. It followed us over from the last tunnel, and looking at it directly causes my stomach to churn, causes the demon in my head to scream, too.

As I hear the demon inside me cry out in agony, begging me to "*Look away*," I choose to continue staring. I want the demon to hurt, even if it means losing my sanity. No matter how sick I feel, I'll keep looking.

Tyrick begins losing his mind. He raises his rifle, aiming it at the back of Sergeant Onaem's head, and—

Sergeant Kusinon bangs his rifle's buttstock against the side of Tyrick's head. Tyrick falls unconscious and hits the floor. When Sergeant Vladik picks him up by the back of his uniform and begins to drag him away, Kusinon grabs his arm and says, "No. Not right now. If he wakes up, we'll need him to be ready."

Vladik grunts in response, then he throws Tyrick's body behind Angoli, who's at the back of the formation. At the same time, Dong-Sun notices that I haven't broken my gaze; he glares at me and says, "You can't lead us. I don't know why the fuck they put you in front—move!"

Dong-Sun pushes me out of the way and asks Kusinon, "How do we kill this thing? I'm sick of looking at it."

Kusinon, who's paled over, glances at everyone holding a camera and says, "Bomb it. Hit the icon on your pads that looks like shrapnel and blow it up. Do it right now."

They follow his orders, and, with a simple touch, three drones burst on the inside of the room. They explode and shake the ground so hard that I have to lean on the wall to keep my balance.

Bach screams, "Fuck yeah!" and pumps his fist in the air before he pats Vladik on the back and says, "That was great!"

Vladik smiles back, and Kusinon points at us all as he grins and tells us, "That's how you surprise the enemy, everyone: with a boom!"

"Let me see," Bach takes Stegan's remote control from him and peers into a screen which displays nothing but smoke.

Meanwhile, I look into the smog covering Dong-Sun's screen, waiting patiently for it to pass. Thick clouds blur and dissolve into a layer which becomes thinner and thinner. Beneath the smog, blackened horns reveal themselves. The eyes of the Ajalu glow with a deep, dark light, glimmering back under a haunting glare. It looks back at all of us, looks right into our souls.

Kusinon's expression goes blank. His body stiffens up, then he turns the barrel of his assault rifle on himself.

"Wait," Bach screams, "what the hell—"

Kusinon shoots himself in the head. He hits the ground at my feet, and blood leaks from his skull to gather at my heels. The formation around me breaks as everyone surrounds Kusinon's body while looking to the other sergeants for answers.

"Dammit!" Vladik exclaims while taking Stegan's camera and preparing to smash it against the ground.

Sergeant Bach stops him by grabbing his arm and says, "Wait! It doesn't matter—we can just run that thing through! There's only one enemy, so let's send our guys in and have them blast it in the head!"

"We can't kill that thing!" Vladik screams at him. He drops the camera and walks away from us, saying, "It's pointless! I couldn't even look it in the eyes—we should pull back."

"We can't,"—Bach grabs him—"get a hold of yourself. Look at what kind of example you're setting for them! Dong-Sun," he says while turning to the soldier at the head of our formation, "do you think you can take that goat-headed bastard?"

"It's no problem, Sergeant," Dong-Sun replies with an empty expression while shaking out the tension in his shoulders. "Send me in."

Sergeant Bach nods and grins. "Good boy," he says. "Everybody get back into formation! Get to the side of the door and I'll unlock it. Sergeant Onaem, what's your status?"

Over where fifteen black chips spin and glow with lines of glowing netite, a stream of red, oval particles condenses and forms what looks like a ruby sheath around Onaem's right arm. In his left, he downs another beer and tosses aside a second empty bottle when he's finished. "I'm almost ready," he says.

"All right," Bach nods while forcefully moving Vladik to face us all while we line up at the side of the door. "We can do this—*you* can do this. I'm unlocking the door now."

We hear a "click" and he says, "Light 'em up."

"Yes Sergeant!" Dong-Sun screams with more heart than the rest of us.

The metal door swings ajar. Dong-Sun rushes inside with the rest of us following right behind him. Dong-Sun charges into the brightly-lit chamber, turns to the right—

A giant boulder plows into him. Cragged rock, tall as a small mountain, slams into Dong-Sun's armor. His Ethernic Cable bursts with all the energy it can muster, and then his suit explodes with a fiery light as the boulder crushes him beneath it. The force of it knocks me back, but Stegan curses and promptly pushes me forward in time to catch a glimpse of Dong-Sun's body being turned into a red pulp.

Behind the great rock, a grotesque, flabby titan with pale white skin and mounds of fat spasms all over while pushing the object forward. It growls and screams as it pushes and pushes, then it smashes the boulder against the far end of the wall. The rock splits in two. The pale giant turns while carrying half of it in one hand. While I aim my pistol at its glob-like face, Stegan and Aro jump into the fray and fire at its great, round stomach. Behind them, Horokaida steps out of the way to let Syra lob a grenade; as the grenade's in flight, Aro shoots it in the air: it explodes, tearing off a chunk of the titan's chin and exposing black, rotted flesh which bleeds out onto the ground.

In response, it hurls the chunk of rock with titanic strength and with a growl that shakes the whole room. Aro and Stegan both use their jet boots, one darting left while the other darts right. The rest of us in the formation follow behind Stegan as he dashes toward the center of the room. The rock chunk crashes into the entrance of the chamber and strikes Sergeant

Bach just as he's about to run farther forward. Bach's turned to paste, and the chunk breaks off into smaller debris that scatters all over the room. As Aro rushes to move out of the way, a large piece of debris bashes in his leg; Aro cries out but uses his propulsion jets to spring himself in our direction.

The titan rushes in behind him with the other chunk of rock in his hand. As Aro issues a shrill scream, the giant behind him slams the slab of rock into the ground—

And Aro escapes. Aro escapes, and the ground opens up in front of our formation. Stegan roars and shoots down at a colossal hand that reaches up with an open palm. The palm closes, and Stegan's body is crushed beneath sparks of red along with a great burst of blood. The horned Ajalu lowers its left fingers, and the giant hand sinks below the crater.

At the same moment, a sniper round pierces the kneecap of the pale titan, prompting it to turn around as it growls. Ein Bira's quick to react: she soars to the far right of the room as the beast lurches toward her. Sergeant Vladik appears at the entrance just as the titan passes by. He crouches down and fires a volley of sapphire-hued energy in its direction. Vladik's shot shears through the muscles on the beast's left leg, forcing it to keel over for a moment before it turns once again to charge at him. Syra and Angoli cover our rear flank by firing their assault rifles into the rolled, pallid flesh of the beast. Horokaida, without jet propulsion boots, cries out, "I'll take the devil in the corner," and begins charging in the goat Ajalu's direction. Aro starts to follow behind him, but he slows down unexpectedly as I begin to pass him up, and then...

Aro faints.

"Soldier down," Angoli screams.

"I've got him," Syra calls out before grabbing Aro, picking him up off the ground, and charging forward.

While Angoli and I move with Horokaida, Sergeant Vladik and Ein work together at the back of the room. Ein fires another round through the pale titan's other kneecap; Vladik fires a second blast at the same kneecap, simultaneously destroying his own weapon with the strength of the blast and the leg of his target. The great titan's brought down, but it continues to move forward at a rapid crawl. Vladik's eyes go wide before he's forced to fly out of the grasp of the beast, then he moves to rejoin those of us at the front of the room as we take on the goat Ajalu.

Ein, taking the initiative, climbs atop the pale titan's back, presses the barrel of her sniper rifle into its head, and blows a burst of grey and black liquid across the floor before leaping off the giant and making a run for it as its corpse collapses onto the ground.

As Syra moves Aro's body closer to the entrance of the next chamber, Horokaida, Angoli, and I lead the way while Ein and Sergeant Vladik trail behind us. Horokaida raises his hammer over his head as he's the first to rush the Ajalu. The demon in my head says, "*He won't make it,*" and I call out for him to stop. From behind, Ein fires a round which races past Horokaida and soars directly at the Ajalu's forehead.

The goat's hands suddenly spring open; its eyes grow wide with black flames; it bares shining white fangs, and it claps its palms together just as the bullet makes contact with its head.

Out from the back of its skull comes spiked, grey hair that extends out like an aura and wraps itself around the front of its head in a great mane. This mane fuses with the dark fur of its face, creating a vortex between two eyes that shimmer like two pale lights; this vortex eats the sniper round, and the Ajalu raises both palms skyward.

The great mane rises above a second head, one that looks like it's made of stone and displays an expression of both terror and hate etched above a broad, stone beard. The grey body of a colossal beast breaks through the ground and extends up with two pairs of arms broken inward and set above rows of insect-like legs that writhe about in all directions. A massive titan struggles to pull its entire body out of the ground but stops short when its first head make contact with the ceiling above it. It quickly keels over and unleashes a howl which sounds like the shrill, distorted scream of a goat mixed with a man's voice.

From this scream, there bellows wind with enough force to knock the three of us backward. Syra, who's already dropped Aro off at the next door, begins firing at the thing, and it reacts by swinging one of its lower legs in her direction. When Syra ducks, it crashes into the wall behind her and, despite it failing to break through, causes the entire chamber to quake.

Syra soars just out of its reach, and Ein fires a round into the left eye of the second head. Fragments of stone fall away, and the second face shifts and spasms as it bares its teeth in rage. The first head roars again, sending forth a blast of wind which almost pushes me off my feet.

"*It's over,*" says the demon in my head, "*none of us will escape. You foul humans walked us right into a trap—you should've turned back! I'll punish you for this, Brock. I'll make you remember* her *again. Over and over. Until you break.*"

I force back its voice in time to see Sergeant Vladik nervously approach with his rifle. We make eye contact, and he glowers at me as he says, "Don't fucking look at me. Kill that thing!"

While I fire in futility with my pistol, Vladik shoots into the open void of the beast's first head. At that very instant, Tyrick suddenly reappears and rejoins our squad in a conscious state once again; the three of us fire in unison while Ein dashes toward the back of the room.

The giant beast twists its muscled abdomen, and, with an arm which looks mangled and broken beyond repair, it swings down at Angoli. Angoli rushes out from under the blow just before it lands and smashes a crater into the ground behind her. Angoli moves toward those of us at the front half of the room and shouts, "Horokaida! Climb on my back now!"

Horokaida races toward her, but the massive titan twists its body once more, just enough to send down the back of its right hand. Its hand crashes into the space separating Angoli and Horokaida, then it sweeps left to hit Angoli. Her Ethernic Cable lights up as she's pushed to the side and thrown off her feet. Angoli flies and hits the west wall of the room; her suit gives out as she makes contact with solid netite and falls to the floor without a sound.

Sergeant Vladik pales over and mutters out loud, "We can't—w-we can't kill this thing. It's impossible."

"*Run*," says the demon in my head.

Vladik responds as though he hears it, and he retreats while leaving the rest of us behind to shoot at a beast that won't go down. It raises all of its arms at once, and Horokaida is the next to retreat, shouting, "Let's go! It's gonna swing at all of us!"

Four palms come together over five pairs of segmented arms; in their wake, the air around them stirs and soars toward us. Nine arms swing at me and the others making a run for it, and I hear the demon in my head begin to shout that we won't make it. Not this time.

To my left, a scarlet figure speeds past like a red blur headed in the opposite direction. Blinding white lights come to life in lines etched across a suit of armor that's marked by pronounced blocks which extend from its shoulders, elbows, kneecaps, and fists. A black faceplate covers a broad head decorated with a white mane flowing behind it; in between each black, netite-lined square, shining red plates decorate the suit's arms, legs, and main torso.

Modukai Sergeant Onaem, geared up in a miniature mech suit, rushes in to absorb the pressure of nine arms. Each one collapses in on him, and his suit explodes outward with a ruby light, showering needle-like sparks in all directions. He raises two bulky arms in the air and generates enough force to push back the grasp of his opponent. Each hand flies backward, and the colossal Ajalu is forced to twist its body in order to regain its momentum. It moves one palm behind its head, then it swings at Onaem with the back of its hand.

Onaem kneels, generates energy like flowing scarlet into the block of netite at the end of his right arm, and punches the Ajalu's hand as soon as it connects.

The Ajalu's giant hand is severed at the wrist, its arm bends inward, and it roars before swinging with both of its remaining right hands. Two palms move downward to crush Onaem in place; Onaem squares up his stance, then he punches up with both netite blocks to produce two bursts of blood-colored energy. Before the Ajalu's strikes can connect, the mech suit shoots out two explosions of power strong enough to sever each hand!

Sergeant Onaem rushes forward, and each step he takes causes the ground beneath us to rumble. He prepares to jump, sending all of his strength into his lower body, and—

The Ajalu swings out with its lower arms and tries to push Onaem off his feet. Onaem reacts in time to turn and puts his blocked fists up just as four spindly appendages crash into his body.

This time, his whole suit lights up with a shower of ruby sparks as it's forced back several feet. In turn, Onaem shoots forth enough energy to stop the attack in its place. At once, Sergeant Vladik, Tyrick, and I fire at both faces belonging to the great beast; Ein fires another round which pierces the right eye of the second face; Syra runs to Horokaida's side and urges him to climb up on her back. He does as she says, and, while the Ajalu moves its left side to bring down each hand that's still attached, Syra flies Horokaida upward and above the amputated wrist of one of the left arms of the beast.

Rather than absorb the full force of the blow, Sergeant Onaem uses the power of his suit to spring himself off the ground and dashes toward the far end of the wall. Behind him, the entire left side of the Ajalu's body crashes down with enough power to knock everyone, including Onaem, off their feet. While Onaem tumbles over onto the ground, Horokaida flies closer and closer to the Ajalu's first head.

From within the dark void between the wispy, grey hairs around it, a sickly-looking face appears and extends outward with the help of a long, bodiless neck. The face of a skinless goat creeps out from the darkness, looking ahead with black eyes and whispering yet speaking loudly enough for everyone to hear sounds that make my body shudder.

I can't think clearly, but my fear spreads like a wildfire. The demon in my head's crying is muffled by the sound of my own heartbeat; I see the face of the goat begin to change and flow into the scenery around it, like a haunting visage wishing to spread as if it were a plague.

Horokaida hollers at the top of his lungs; an aura flows from his body while he's perched atop Syra's shoulders. When he sees the goat's dark visage looking up at him, he growls through his fear.

—SHUNGEJ—

Horokaida brings down his hammer as his arms expand. He smashes his target's head into a mess of ink-black blood as his hammer tears through flesh and bone, rending apart the true head of the Ajalu. Using his full strength forces him to fall from Syra's back, but she promptly flies down and grabs him underneath his right arm before flying away as the second head begins to collapse into stone fragments. As dust and debris break away at the bottom, dark blood spurts out from within the void belonging to the first head.

The body of the giant Ajalu slowly keels over with a sullen moan which hums throughout the chamber. Just as it tries to stop its first head from hitting the floor, Sergeant Onaem rushes in, punches forward, and sends a blast of red energy into the dark void. The punch carries enough power to set its grey mane aflame, and it sends forth a ray of ruby light to incinerate the head within it.

The Ajalu's death knell is muffled by the sound of the blast, and its massive body falls with a powerful thud while nearly covering the full length of the room. Onaem climbs up onto its back and punches one final blast of energy into its head, causing it to explode and burst with dark blood. He rests his shoulders back and sighs while staring up at the ceiling. "Whew," he exclaims, "that felt good!"

Sergeant Onaem looks around the room, then he says, "Everyone, gather around me. Brock, bring Aro over here; Syra, grab Angoli."

"Roger," both of us respond and hurry back with our comrades in tow. As I try to set Aro down, he suddenly wakes up and panics. Aro looks around in shock, and then, when he sees me, he scowls and punches me in the face before pushing me away as he gets up.

Ein catches him doing this and points her sniper rifle at his head while Horokaida grabs him by his uniform. "Don't hit him again," Horokaida growls at him, and Aro complies with a curt nod.

Syra slaps Angoli's face, but Angoli remains unconscious. Her Ethernic Cable's burned out, and Syra tries to wake her again by pouring out some of the water in her canteen over Angoli's head. There's still no response, so Onaem tells her, "Leave it. She'll wake up." Syra bows her head and then stands in rank with the rest of us.

"Take a knee," Onaem orders, and seven of us kneel while facing him in a straight row. With his voice amplified by his suit of armor, Onaem begins to instruct us:

"This is called a 'Mach Dozer,' also known as the 'Red Suit.' It's one of the seven mechs used by Enrec and the only one we've got—hiccup, excuse me—the only one we've got until we reach the next checkpoint."

"We're fucked," Sergeant Vladik interrupts and shakes his head as he says, "We have to try to go back."

"*He's right,*" says the demon occupying my head. "*You made me suffer, Brock. You kept going when I told you to stop, and I'm going to punish you for that. Just wait and see. I know all about Kalina.*"

"Ahem," Onaem clears his throat and looks to Vladik as he says, "Sergeant, shut the hell up. We've got a long way to go and plenty of soldiers willing to give their best efforts at getting there. If you discourage them now—hiccup—we're gonna lose everything."

Sergeant Onaem triggers a mechanism on the inside of his suit which temporarily parts his helmet and exposes his face. He points at Vladik's duffel bag and says, "Now give me another beer."

While shaking, Vladik does as he says and quietly returns to his position. Onaem continues:

"We're going to use the rest of the drones we have to scout out the next few areas, but we won't be blowing up any more of them. Nah," he says while gesturing for Sergeant Vladik to come closer, "we'll take a smarter approach from here on out, and, now that we're down to fewer recruits and less gear, using more powerful weapons won't affect our tactics as much."

Sergeant Vladik hands Onaem his duffel, and Onaem rummages through it before taking out a short, black axe which he throws to Aro. He reaches in again and takes out what looks like half of a dark katana with a flat point at its end and a bright green light at its edges. Onaem tosses it to Syra before reaching in once more and retrieving a black object in the shape of a staff; it folds outward and into a harpoon with three green arrows attached to its sides, and Onaem hands it to Sergeant Vladik. Again, he reaches inside and brings out half of a dark spear, and the other half extends itself out into a glowing red point as he gives it to Tyrick.

Aro twists the handle of his axe and causes it to grow in length while powering on with patterns of blue light etched into its body beneath an aura of steam blooming around it; within her grasp, Syra's blade grows to twice its length while giving off heat which can be felt from a close distance. Onaem takes one look around at each of us and explains, "I gave Aro what's called a 'sonic axe.' Each stroke of the weapon should send out sound waves capable of bursting eardrums and disrupting enemy movements. Syra has a 'heat blade,' and that thing should be able to cut through any monster we run into. Sergeant Vladik's got a harpoon with three rounds; each one will burn through the weapon itself, but they contain small explosions of plasma primed for detonation on contact. Last but not least, Tyrick's got a netite spear; it moves faster than you'd think, and a well-timed thrust should pierce through armor more easily than a sniper round would."

"What about us, Sergeant?" Horokaida asks with more bravery than the rest of our formation.

"What about you?" Onaem rephrases the question while raising his eyebrows. "You can shut the fuck up," he says while pointing at Horokaida's weapon, "that hammer was good enough to take care of the last beast, so what are you worried about? Do you wanna do more pushups?"

Horokaida gestures with his thumb at me and asks, "What about him? What about Angoli?"

As Angoli regains consciousness and wakes up with rapid breaths and a disorientated look on her face, Sergeant Onaem shrugs his shoulders.

"They're both probably going to die. I gave our best weapons to the best soldiers we've got left, recruit. Brock was supposed to be the first one in the room to die, and Angoli passed out before she could be very useful. If we're going to take on Alandra," he says, "then we need better soldiers than those two."

Horokaida doesn't respond and looks down at the ground. When he doesn't say anything else, Sergeant Onaem snorts and continues with a smirk, "You've all just gotten a taste of what the battlefield will be like once Enrec launches its first major attack against Alandra. There are no excuses for weakness; there is no forgiveness. If you fail here, it's because you're too weak. If you fucked up, then we've already given up on you because there's no reason to waste government resources on recruits who can't make the cut. Brock and Angoli have already let us down, so we have to let more reliable soldiers take the lead on this next venture.

"Enrec can't promise you successful missions," he says. "It can't even promise you safe training exercises; we train as we fight, and, if you ruin your chances here, there's nothing we can do for you. Instead, fight harder and stop being so weak; we can't use weak people.

"We're going to go ahead and move on from this point. Don't focus on the dead, recruits. Leave those who've failed behind you because focusing on the lost will only make you more distracted. Rank no longer makes a difference at this moment, for everything we do now as a team has to count. In the rooms to follow, there'll be more pain, more death. There's no telling what will happen, and, shit, we might all fail.

"Let's fight on anyway."

8
Despair

--

Brock

--

I CAN FEEL ANOTHER MEMORY COMING BACK ON ITS OWN. I can feel it coming, but I have to stop it. Private Ronas… he passed.

He passed, and then the same people who'd hurt him wanted to hurt me. A week after returning back to our base of operations, one of my sergeants asked me to grab a "file" for him out of a secluded room. I went into that room, and there they were. Ten soldiers, half of them grinning and half of them staring hard at me with blank expressions.

"It's your fault," one of them said. "Go ahead, say it. Tell us that it's your fault, Brock. Say it."

--

We send three drones beyond the red, metal door and into the following room.

Nothing. Three cameras clear a chamber of clear white tiles lined with grey. Sergeant Onaem hesitates before giving us the 'okay' to pass through, and then our squad of nine moves into the empty chamber and on to yet another door that's the color of blood.

At this door, Onaem's Mach Dozer gives off a series of sparks punctuated by him cursing, "Shit!"

"That's not good," Sergeant Vladik mutters to himself.

Onaem shakes his head and says, "Shut up. It'll crush them if they find out; it's too early for this to be happening."

Vladik gestures toward the drones, "Should we send them in?"

Onaem hesitates, then he says, "Yeah. Go ahead."

Again, we conduct surveillance by sending each one through, and, on the other side of the door, a blinding white light obscures the entire chamber. I look at Aro's screen to watch a broad, pale expanse clear and shrink down into a room which could only fit around ten people altogether.

A lone body sits at the center of this room. White contrasts with grey skin which has the texture of stone covered in spots with black dirt. I see a bald head and an eyeless face. I see torn, empty sockets hanging above a dark, toothless grin. A smile creeps across its jaw, running from ear to ear as it bares a void which floats between shriveled lips. Below the head is a body so emaciated that its ribcage presses out completely, as if its skeleton only shows itself to compensate for a total lack of fat or muscle.

While seated in a grim form of meditation, an eyeless being grins back at us through each of our cameras. When meeting its gaze for the first time, the demon in my head begins to scream at me; it curses my name, runs through images of every memory I've ever tried to repress throughout my life, and sets a fire burning within my head.

Within that dark smile, an aura flickers, bursting outward; Aro's camera shuts off.

"What the fuck," I hear Onaem utter as he begins shaking his remote. "It didn't even hit us—hey," he looks over at Vladik, who holds up the black screen belonging to the third and last camera and stops short of asking if his works. "That doesn't make any sense," he says.

Onaem taps his screen more rapidly, but it doesn't respond. Through his suit, I see him shrug his shoulders with a great sigh, then he utters, "I need another beer."

"When we get in there," he says while pointing at the door, "I'm fucking that thing up. If it just messed up the last drones we've got, then I'm pissed. Let me go in first—Sergeant Vladik!"

"Got it," Vladik replies while hurrying to unlock the door.

Sergeant Vladik opens the portal, and a dark cloud spills out.

"Don't pass through, Brock. DON'T DO IT!"

I ignore the demon and choose to walk directly behind Sergeant Onaem as I do. Instead of letting me follow behind him, though, Sergeant Vladik pushes me out of the way, shouting, "Move, you fucking loser!"

As Vladik readies his harpoon, Tyrick also cuts me off and says, "What the hell are you gonna do, huh? Why are you even coming?"

"I'm here to die like the rest of you," I tell him. "Just let me do my part and I'll let you do yours."

Tyrick looks away and grunts in response, and, as a unit, the rest of us proceed with Sergeant Onaem leading the way.

I expect to pile into a crowded room, but, as we pass beyond the next door, the white sheen from before gives way to grey and white clouds above us. From what looks like a normal sky, blood-colored snow rains down as if it were red tears falling from heaven. Red tears blend with red and yellow leaves that fall from twisted trees with wood the color of maroon. Tears, leaves, and dirt mix to form a pool of shallow, red water at our feet, and, far ahead, pale wind blows back at us in the shape of a familiar face. The meditating Ajalu from before taunts us with images of its head forming, dissipating, and re-forming, blasting forth a gale of wind strong enough to slow down Onaem's Mach Dozer.

"Why won't you listen to me! Why won't you turn back?"

When I don't respond to the demon, he forces the image of Kalina into my head once again. This time... this time it really hurts.

--

I didn't want it when she wanted it. Kalina started getting more forceful. When I refused, she pressed again and again; she started wanting to do it in front of our kid.

"It's not right for her to see this," I said. "Let her go back to her room."

Kalina slapped me and grinned. "Why not? Why don't you show her how it's done?"

I felt anger well up within me, but I wouldn't strike her.

I picked up our daughter and carried her to her room. Kalina began hitting me as I did, and Alina cried. Alina was confused, and I wouldn't let her see this. When I shut the door to our daughter's room, Kalina hit me harder and harder.

"Why don't you want it when I do?" she screamed. "What, are you looking at some other bitch now? Who are you cheating on me with, Brock? Who is it,"—she punched me in the face while baring her teeth—"tell me who that whore is or I'll bring Alina out here again and make her watch me shoot you! Would you like that? Huh?" she asked again with a slap.

I'm trying to remember, trying to remember what happened after that, but...

--

"Brock?" Horokaida nudges my shoulder. "You good?"

The ground below us heaves and sighs, rolling progressively into a hill. Aro pushes me from behind and says, "Hurry up before you ruin the formation!"

"Hey," Horokaida yells at him, "chill out. He's remembering something. What is it?"

"It's... it's nothing," I reply while looking down.

"*Oh, it's something. Let me pry just a little further. I want to see what a puny wretch you are. Let me look, closer and closer.*"

"No!" I shout out loud.

"*What did you do to those men, huh? If you don't tell me, I'll finish your memory with Kalina. I want to know what she did to you, too. I want to know everything.*"

"Calm down," Horokaida says with a nervous smile. "You look like you're losing it."

"Brock," I hear Ein ask from the back of the formation, "what's wrong?"

Before I can answer, Onaem stops ahead of us to exclaim, "Oh my god."

"What? What is it," Vladik panics while moving to the side of Onaem as he looks over the horizon.

Once he does, Vladik mutters, "No. No!" He shakes his head and starts to turn back, but Sergeant Onaem grabs him and says, "Wait. Don't back down. Not yet."

Up ahead, I see it.

A great blooming shadow with the head of a bull. Skin like a dark shroud blots out its face, showing only the silhouette of a horned skull towering above a torso which spreads out into ripples the color of ink. A massive body surges toward us like black waves led by a faceless demon. As it moves, the ground beneath us shudders. I hear a deep howl which echoes across the field and becomes a constant, throaty hum, growing louder and louder in rhythm with the angry demon inside of my head, who screams for me to run.

"*I'll make you remember what you did,*" it warns. "*TURN BACK NOW!*"

"Sergeant Vladik," Onaem says quietly, "take the shot."

Vladik crouches down while shaking and tries to steady his aim.

"Hurry up before it gets too close."

As the bull-headed Ajalu courses into full view, the dark ripples below it become eyeless eels with shining white teeth; each time one of them writhes and shoots out in our direction, jet-black liquid froths from their mouths and bodies. Above them, a shadowy mist obscures a bulky, rigid upper body. The horned skull bears down on us; Vladik takes the first shot.

A shining green bolt shoots forth from Vladik's harpoon and flies toward the center of the Ajalu's skull. As it ascends and descends, the bolt lands below its head and strikes at its throat. Green static fills the sky, then it converges into the pulsation of an emerald wave; in the wake of this pulsation, energy explodes outward into a blast which covers the whole of the Ajalu and colors the clouds above with a neon tint.

In response, the black skin of its neck parts and shoots out a face which reaches us like a ghost extending itself to show the twisted snare of a wolf-like head; its snout bends around yellow teeth and bares warped eyes with black pupils too large for its face. I hear a howl that makes my ears ring and blots out my vision with a white screen. The demon in my head cries for mercy, but Vladik's cries are even worse.

The ghost disappears behind an ominous wall of black eels which inches ever closer. I look to my right and see a vein popping out of Sergeant Vladik's head as he screams while flushing red all over.

"Pull yourself together!" Onaem shouts, "It's not that bad—shoot it again!"

When Vladik fails to respond, choosing instead to hold his head as he screams words that I don't understand, Sergeant Onaem tears Vladik's weapon from his grasp. Onaem's suit makes a clinking noise as he crouches down while yet another spark shoots out of his shoulder socket. Sergeant Onaem readies a second bolt, Vladik screams, "No!" and Onaem fires another round at the Ajalu.

This time, the bolt lands square atop the Ajalu's skull, exploding with an emerald light as a roar echoes out from the wall of black shadows. Another face stretches toward us and screams as it exposes four red slits for eyes lining its forehead and three rows of teeth. Scarlet light shimmers and covers the expanse of its head, forcing Onaem to hesitate as he stands tall while staring down the giant beast.

"I can't take it! I can't!" Vladik screams as the vein in his forehead bulges out even further. He covers his head with one hand and rushes toward the back of the formation before Onaem can stop him.

As Sergeant Onaem loads the final bolt, and, as I look behind me, I notice that Vladik's running toward someone in particular.

He's running toward Ein.

Sergeant Onaem pauses to aim, then he pulls the trigger. The harpoon explodes in his hands and causes his entire suit to react with a burst of red energy. I smell burning as the exterior of his suit smolders, but the Mach Dozer's hard shell absorbs the blast.

"Help me!" I hear Ein's voice from behind.

"Let's go!" Onaem demands while charging ahead.

Instead of following him, I turn back. Tyrick reaches out to stop me, but I push away his hand and move toward Ein.

Sergeant Vladik's grabbing Ein by the neck and trying to rip her collar open. "Stop fighting it," he shouts, "it's all over anyway! Let me have you now!"

"Sergeant," Horokaida starts to talk Vladik down while trying to pull him off Ein, "what are you—"

Sergeant Vladik punches Horokaida in the face and grabs Ein by the neck while she glares back at him with a cold expression. "Don't touch me again, recruit! We're all about to die—don't you see it? Let me have her!"

I walk up to the side of Sergeant Vladik. Ein makes eye contact with me, and I shoot Vladik in the head. Blood sprays from his right temple, and Vladik's body hits the ground while Horokaida stares at me in shock.

"You know what you just did, right?"

I reply with a nod. Ein says nothing and chooses to look down instead before she leaves us to retrieve her weapon.

"That was treason, Brock. You just killed one of our leaders."

We look at each other for a moment, and then—

A dark body flies before my eyes and screams as it soars through the air.

Grey, stone skin covering a fanged infant whisks by with small, feathered wings fluttering behind it. A demonic child crashes into the ground with an ear-piercing screech and explodes into a pool of black blood.

To my left, I spot a second Ajalu. I see a tall, skeletal body that's curved at the upper end of its torso and with blackened ribs spread too far apart. Rather than legs, its lower ribs extend downward and become spindles of bone, propelling it above the ground as a dozen fanged infants hover around its eyeless skull in an oval. Each infant has dark eyes shaped like horns. Their mouths all hang agape with rows of jagged teeth befitting dark voids that echo with the cries of undead children.

The Ajalu floating at the center of the ring points at Angoli with the only finger it has on its hand, and one fanged infant soars toward her with speed that she can't track. Horokaida tackles Angoli, and the two of them hit the ground as the demonic child screeches above them.

Far past Angoli and Horokaida, Sergeant Onaem charges the bull-headed Ajalu while Tyrick follows in tow. Onaem calls out to Tyrick just as one of the giant eels rushes toward him: "Attack its head!"

As Tyrick staggers his stance, his spear becomes aglow with a sapphire light. Tyrick lunges and thrusts his spear forward: it extends outward and rapidly, flying toward the great beast without ever stopping short. The point of the spear strikes the Ajalu's head and emits a pulse of blue static.

Black energy radiates back down the length of the spear, causing it to shake and waver while Tyrick freezes on the spot. Rather than move, he remains fixed in place as a giant pale head projects from the top of the Ajalu's body. Beady, puckered eyes hang over a scowl filled with knives for teeth; an oval head stretches forth to scream at Tyrick, and Tyrick begins to run as soon as his spear returns to its original size.

Aro stops him, shouting, "Hey! You can't just leave!" Tyrick brushes him off and pushes him away while fleeing toward the back of the formation. Rather than chase him, Aro takes Tyrick's place, grips his axe with both hands as static gathers around its head, and swings with fury which shoots forth into waves of sound. Each wave breaks the sound barrier, screeching through the air while traveling toward the head of black bull. When the colossal Ajalu attempts to project another face, it's immediately forced back as ripples of sound cause its entire form to quake.

The bull-headed Ajalu sends forth one of its eels to lunge at Onaem, but the force of each soundwave causes its slime-covered body to turn and writhe as it moves to strike Onaem's Mach Dozer.

Sergeant Onaem plows into the head of the eel with a hard punch, blowing it back with an earthquake of a hit which resonates throughout its body while causing it to compress under a hateful snarl. At the same moment, a second dark eel lunges at Onaem, and he punches with his other hand. Onaem blows its head back while searing away most of its face, exposing only its lower jaw beneath the charred remains of a sunken head.

Aro takes a deep breath and then swings so hard that his Ethernic Cable gives out with a series of bright sparks: five soundwaves rocket into the body of the titan, and five shaken eels spring toward Onaem in a mad rush. Sergeant Onaem charges headfirst into his first target, and the strength of his charge blows back one dark worm as the others clamp their jaws around the arms and legs of the Mach Dozer.

"Tyrick, help me out here!" Aro screams while getting into position once again.

Ein suddenly fires a round at the head of the bull, and it reels back just as a scarlet light gathers around the body of Onaem's mechanized suit. The colossal Ajalu slowly begins to lower its head so that two narrow horns ascend above a dark, eyeless expanse which meets the earth and forms a black hole that crawls closer and closer. Amidst the expanse, drooping eyebrows open wide to reveal black pearls for eyes; the beast opens its toothless maw and sends forth a scream which strikes everyone like a fierce gust and raises the voice of the demon in my head to a high-pitched wail.

Sergeant Onaem's Mach Dozer gives off a burst of ruby-colored energy, and I hear him roar just as he punches out with both hands and fires blasts of scorching heat into the two eels above him; I hear him roar again as he stomps both feet downward and smashes the heads of the eels below him. Dark worms burst into liquefied flesh around a scarlet aura. Onaem's Mach Dozer begins to heat up and glow with a scorching red. Just as a dozen more eels surge in his direction, Sergeant Onaem, beneath a dozen sparks to match them, issues a battle cry which pierces the air around us.

"One last time," he shouts. "One last time—this is it, and I'll give it everything I've got!"

Sergeant Onaem charges toward the colossal Ajalu as it continues to scream. Against the force of the next gust of wind that it bellows, the Mach Dozer becomes a blaze of red.

"ARO," I hear him call out, "SWING ONE LAST TIME!"

Aro begins to swing as power compresses into the head of his axe. He tightens his grip, rotates his upper body, and prepares to strike!

And then a fanged infant connects with his head.

The infant bites down, grey mixes with the color of blood, and Aro's head is torn from his shoulders as red sprays from the hole in his neck.

"Aro!" Tyrick screams in terror while looking toward the second Ajalu. Just as it sends another fanged devil his way, Tyrick ducks and thrusts the point of his spear through the skeletal Ajalu's chest: blue sparks fly from a sphere of power which explodes out and incinerates three of the infants floating above it along with half of its torso.

Just as the Ajalu poises itself to throw two more of its spawn, Syra appears behind it. Syra's blade emits steam followed by flames spouting from both sides; Syra swings, and she decapitates the Ajalu, forcing the head of a pale spirit to fly up and shriek as it drifts into the air. When its body continues to stand in place, with all of its remaining spawn sinking into a dark puddle along the ground, Angoli unleashes a barrage from her assault rifle and pierces its body through while forcing out the rest of its pale essence. The headless monster breaks into fragments and then splits apart into debris that becomes a grey liquid as it touches the ground.

As Angoli finishes off one abomination, I rush toward the other and pick up Aro's sonic axe. While Onaem continues dashing toward the colossal Ajalu up ahead, I gather energy once again into the head of the weapon, then I swing with all the strength that I can muster.

Fierce soundwaves echo out, striking both Onaem's suit and the great body of the dark beast. While the Mach Dozer shoots out sparks from all over, the force of the swing causes the colossal Ajalu's black wall to shudder. It opens its maw even wider, and Onaem rushes in.

Onaem's mech suit transforms into a meteor that blasts its way past each writhing eel head and shoots into the void belonging to the Ajalu's mouth. Sergeant Onaem springs forward with one punch, and, with that punch, he generates all the energy remaining within his suit; Onaem becomes a supernova, bursting outward in a blaze of red which takes up the entire body of the beast with a fiery light.

Below the gloom of the forest of clouds overhead, I see what looks like a molten sun blasting a rift through tides of darkness. Bright scarlet light becomes blindingly brilliant above the hollow scream of a forlorn titan. Its dark body is seared into a liquid ocean which spreads across the field underneath the light of a flaming red suit. From where I stand, I feel a heatwave cover the air around me. I smell burning metal and see the head of Onaem poking out from a mesh of red and grey.

The Mach Dozer has melted partway and drains across Onaem's right shoulder while exposing his head as well as the top left side of his body. What's left of our squad quickly approaches an ocean of black marked with a steaming ruby at its center.

"Yes! That's it! It's time to run now, Brock. Run before I make you remember it—do it now!"

I continue to approach with the others, ignoring the demon's screams as my memories of that night with Kalina return...

--

I didn't give her what she wanted, so she took it.

In the middle of the night, she pressed the cold barrel of a pistol against my head. When I looked up, she was smiling down at me, flashing bright white teeth under eyes that glowed with a hatred which I still don't understand. She beamed a wicked smile down at me, and, when I was fully awake, she hit me across my right temple with the gun. When I didn't pass out from it, her grin got more intense. She rode me when I didn't want it and rode it harder and rougher than I'd ever want it.

She looked down at me and said, "This is mine. If you ever try to take it from me, Brock, I'll kill you. When I want to fuck you, I will. If you say no, I'll kill you."—Kalina hit me with her pistol again—"Do you hear me? Tell me you're listening or I'll shoot you, do you understand?"

"Yes, Kalina," I told her while feeling detached from myself, "I understand."

"It's mine," she said while dropping the gun and wrapping her hands around my neck. Kalina moved her face an inch away from mine and spat, "It's mine and no one else's!"

--

"I hate you," I tell the demon.

"Ah, that feels so good. I can really feel *your pain now. That's right, you're just a stupid tool, Brock. She raped you, cheated on you, then left your child behind. Now poor Alina's gone, and it's all your fault. It's all your fault because you couldn't keep Kalina happy, isn't that right? You've always been a failure."*

"I'm going to kill you," is all I have to say in response.

"Go ahead and tell me about what happened in that room. About what happened with those soldiers. C'mon now."

"No. Stop."

"I'll pull it out of you—oh yes I will. You're going to remember."

As the memory creeps into my head, seeing the exposed face of our squad leader brings me back to reality.

"Don't ignore me!" the demon cries.

I do just that, and I'm conscious when I see Sergeant Onaem make eye contact with all of us and smile. He gives our squad a thumbs up and says, "Looks like I made it after all. I can't feel my body, but I made it."

A moment of silence follows, then Onaem begins to cringe in pain.

"Oh Avva, now it really hurts. I think… I think parts of me got melted down with the suit."

Horokaida takes a knee and bows his head. "Thank you," he says. "You saved everyone."

Sergeant Onaem nods his head with a solemn expression; around him, steam pours out from the liquefied metal draining across what's left of the hard shell of the Mach Dozer. As small flames surround the head of our squad leader, a tall, skeletal body emerges from behind him.

I see a pair of thick, feathery wings wrapped around a grey and white body without legs. A skull missing its lower jaw peers out from between black fur; its wings part to expose hundreds of black bugs covering its ribs and compensating for its lack of flesh.

Four long arms of bare bone wrap themselves around Onaem's body. The winged Ajalu lowers its skull and inhales to create a vacuum which tears at the skin on our squad leader's head.

As Sergeant Onaem begins to scream, pieces of his skull separate as insects are drawn toward the blood that flows behind each piece. Onaem's face is quickly covered by buzzing, black bugs, and he screams, "Kill it! Horokaida! Horokaida!"

Angoli begins to open fire before Horokaida can even stand, but, as soon as the first rounds fly from her rifle, another form in the shape of a tall statue appears behind her. The stone, sculpted body of a pregnant, curly-haired woman with pupil-less eyes and only an open robe to adorn her waves a sword above her head.

Right when Angoli turns, the top half of her is severed below both shoulders; it slides off her torso, and Angoli's body tumbles to the ground in a pool of bright blood.

Syra soars toward the statuesque woman with tears in her eyes. She swings just as Tyrick thrusts at the Ajalu who's devouring Sergeant Onaem's body: the sword-wielding woman flashes to the side, but Tyrick's attack strikes true. While Tyrick pierces the head of the devourer, the female Ajalu rapidly moves her sword up and brings it down to cut open Syra's right shoulder.

Tyrick withdraws his spear, and Horokaida rushes at the devourer with a horizontal swing. Just as his hammer's about to connect, the skeletal beast fades into a faint outline of itself and allows the weapon to pass through it. At the same instant, the statuesque Ajalu flickers by with speed I can't follow and appears behind Horokaida. She thrusts her sword right as a small hand tears a hole in her belly and reaches toward him, but Horokaida ducks and backs away. He backs away, and Ein fires a round into the Ajalu's head, chipping away stone as it turns to look at her.

Tyrick thrusts his spear through the statue's midsection, then he calls out, "Now, Syra!"

Syra appears at the Ajalu's side and swings her blade of scorching flames through the air: she severs the statue's sword arm, but the Ajalu kicks out faster than she can anticipate; it kicks and shatters the right side of her ribcage, prompting Syra to spit up blood before she falls on her back. At that very moment, the skeletal Ajalu from before appears over her and begins to reach down with each of its arms.

Horokaida charges toward the pregnant statue, smashes open its left leg, and rushes on to strike at the second Ajalu; in conjunction with his attack, I swing my sonic axe hard enough to hear its blade break into pieces underneath the pressure that issues out of it, pressure which punches into the body of the stone woman and causes chunks of her to fall to the ground. Ein fires another round which forces the statue's head to explode and results in the rest of its figure bursting into grey dust.

Before the devourer can even touch Syra, she thrusts her blade upward and into its skull; Horokaida simultaneously smashes in its neck, and, together, they dismember the last opponent who engages us. Without a head, the Ajalu disperses into a swarm of flies which surges upward in a loud wave.

All around us, and as Horokaida helps Syra to her feet, the world fades and blends into a white, empty expanse of tiles lined with glowing red.

At once, a strange gas the color of night begins to fill the chamber. Tyrick panics before the rest of us and says, "I don't have a gas mask—someone give me theirs! Please!"

Horokaida reacts quickly and rummages through Vladik's duffel bag before retrieving one of his own; instead of wearing it, though, he offers it to me.

"No thank you," I reply while searching the area for another bag. "I didn't earn it."

When Ein finds a mask that she can wear, Tyrick tries to take it from her. Horokaida pushes him back and then gives his mask to Tyrick. When Tyrick asks, "Are you crazy or something?" Horokaida smirks and replies, "Yeah. If Brock can handle it, then so can I."

"Take Tyrick's mask, Brock. Kill him and take his mask—I can smell it! You can't inhale whatever that is!"

"Shut the hell up," I say to him out loud.

"It'll destroy your mind, Brock! Kill Tyrick and take his mask now!"

I choose not to respond, and, in return, I'm flooded with images of that night, images of my body being used by Kalina when I couldn't decide whether or not I loved her anymore. As I try to move forward and slow down my breathing, that night repeats itself, searing the same vision into my head and forcing pressure throughout my skull.

The five of us press on while a growing mist gathers at our feet. When I catch myself breathing in thick, noxious fumes, I remember the smell of her on that night. I remember her threatening me to stay just as in love with her as before, but I couldn't. I couldn't, and I fought against my own hatred just to stay alive, just to keep her from shooting me.

"Yes, that's it, you bastard. Now you'll feel the same pain I feel! You deserved it. You deserved everything that she did to you."

I remember kicks, punches, headbutts. I remember biting, cursing, stabbing.

I breathe in: pain fills my entire body. I breathe out: pressure leaves my diaphragm and causes my lungs to burn so badly that I can't stand it. I wheeze and cough while my eyes begin to sting and my nose runs. Because I feel so disorientated, I walk ahead of the formation and next to Horokaida, who strides confidently while leading the rest of the pack. Behind me, I hear the muffled breathing of everyone else with a gas mask and begin to feel envy as my skull pounds harder and harder.

"I can make her hurt you again and again. Kalina is pain, Brock, and that's all you're worth. That's all you're worth for making me endure this, and I want you to hate it as much as I hate you. Choke, Brock. Choke and die."

As I start to rub my temples, Horokaida stops us to place his hand on my shoulder and bow his head.

"I never was much into praying," he says, "but I'm going to try something and hope that it works."

Horokaida becomes quiet and glances down while a faint light emits a subtle outline around his body. A thin layer of aura glimmers from a halo surrounding his head and works its way down to spread out and grow in stature.

"Hey, what are you doing?" Tyrick says while stepping toward us both.

"I'm going to make him a promise, that's all," Horokaida responds without looking at either of us.

Ein pulls Tyrick back; when he gasps and tries to fight her, Ein nearly slaps the mask off of his face. Tyrick turns toward Ein and raises his fists, but Syra quickly steps in and raises her blade to his throat while blood drips from the cut on her right shoulder.

Meanwhile, Horokaida begins to pray.

2
Breaking

--

Brock

--

"**D**EAR AVVA, the power you've given me is great, and so allow me to bestow it upon someone else. I vow to make a contract," he states while cutting open the palm of his hand with a knife and drawing blood from mine before shaking my hand with a tight grip, "and let this contract bind us unto death.

"Dear Avva, let Brock embrace the strength of my zol, the light of my soul, and the heart of my strength. Like two brothers in arms, let us share a bond which will ensure that we both make it out of here alive. Let two soldiers become one, marching on until we've seen this mission through to its end.

"Dear Avva, let this contract bind us. Let us survive this hell together."

With those words, I feel the rush of adrenaline spread through me; I feel the onset of sharp, agonizing pain, like my skin and bones are struggling to tear themselves apart. My vision blurs red as blood drains from my eyes and heat rises toward the top of my skull. The pain I feel is washed away by a surge of endorphins; pain's replaced by joy, joy in a hopeless place. The voice of the demon inside me momentarily becomes quiet, and, because it's tried to possess me for as long as it has, I'm able to feel its fear as something powerful emerges from within me.

"Do you sense it, brother?" Horokaida asks.

I nod in response and close my eyes so that I can see my daughter again. All the hate in Kalina's eyes vanishes when I see the face of Alina, who smiles back at me in her hospital bed and holds my hand as she fades away. I sense peace for the first time followed by the serenity of warm energy rushing through my veins. Although I can't see the same aura that surrounds Horokaida, I know that something's changed within me.

Where there was agony and exhaustion, I can breathe clearly in the midst of quiet relaxation.

"I can sense it, too," Ein says and touches my back. "You've changed."

"Why didn't you give that power to me?" Tyrick exclaims in spite of Syra's blade hovering next to his throat. "Why did you give it to that loser? He got everyone killed during the last training exerci—"

"No one cares," Ein replies with a quick glance back in his direction. "Without a squad leader, all we've got is each other now."

"Ugh!" Tyrick brushes Syra aside and begins marching forward without us. "We're doomed," he says as the mist condenses into a deep fog.

The rest of us follow in tow before Horokaida sets the pace by jogging past Tyrick. All five of us go from jogging to running through a growing darkness, with only the brightness of the netite ceiling above to guide us.

When we make it to the next blood-colored door, the atmosphere's punctuated by a deep hum which stops and starts without any set flow or rhythm. Syra touches the side of her head and groans while Ein rests her head against the wall.

"We can't stop here," Horokaida warns us and begins pulling on the handle of the door.

It doesn't budge, and he only pulls harder.

The hum starts and stops again, and then the door unlocks itself. We step through into a white-tiled room lined with glowing red.

At the center, there rests what's now the giantized body of the smiling sage from before. Sunken, grey skin sighs against a massive ribcage and droops down from the craters that constitute its eye sockets, craters so large that undulating, dirt-covered skin stretches deep into a skull of shriveled flesh.

The smiling sage sits in meditation and begins to turn its head to face us. As it does, I hear the sound of bones cracking echo out from this movement. While the rest of the sage stays fixed in place, cold, mocking holes for eyes look down on us as its grin widens. Without uttering a sound, I can hear the noise of an old creature laughing inside of my head; in response, I feel a strange heat burn at the back of my eyes. Dark waves of aura extend out from the body of the sage and press upon our squad while the mist from before gathers around us. Tyrick, Syra, and Ein all get down on their knees and begin to peer up at the sage with hopeless expressions.

Although Horokaida and I can stand the feeling of acidic corrosion biting at our skulls, the being living inside me right now can't bear it anymore.

"You've brought me too far, Brock. You should've given up a long time ago. Enough is enough."

Like flames licking against my forehead before being blown away to leave behind a cold chill, I feel the presence of something drain out of my body. I sense the weight of a deep dread being lifted from my being along with the image of Kalina grinning down at me aside the images of two memories that I'd rather leave behind.

White and red runs like two streams which wrap around each other to combine into the shaken form of an entity seemingly composed of wind and dust. Amidst the gathering fog, another type of mist collects into the shape of a human without features or any bodily definition. A gaseous cloud of two shades creates a figure which stands at the same height that I do, a figure without a mouth, nose, or hair; instead, ruby eyes glare back at me from a ghostlike creature with three horns made of condensed wind hanging down from the back of its skull.

Tyrick looks up from his sunken stupor and exclaims, "It's him. It looks like the loser on our team!"

Horokaida readies his hammer and glances between me and the demon. "Why does it look like you, Brock? Did you summon it?"

Before I can respond, the demon raises its finger to point at me and says, *"Give me the stuffed animal tucked within your pouch. Give me that, and I'll forgive you."*

"What?" I shout in total amazement. "But why do you want that?"

"*It's only fair,*" it replies while tilting its head to one side. "*That little bunny holds every good memory you have left. If you give it to me,*"—the demon gestures for me to hand it over—"*I'll forgive you.*"

Horokaida tenses up and glares at the spirit with me. "Why the hell do you need a stuffed animal to forgive him?" he asks before I can.

Without acknowledging him, the demon continues to stare at me and says without emotion, "*Because your friend has made me suffer much more than I ever wanted to. My name is Ekikon, and I am a master of Imago. Brock didn't have the strength to fight back my intrusions, and he didn't have the strength to protect me against the Ajalus' intrusions, either. Because Brock is a failure in all respects, I demand proper punishment for his inadequacy.*"

"Fuck off," I tell him. "We fought the Ajalu. If you can't, then you never belonged here anyway."

"*GIVE IT TO ME,*" Ekikon screams while generating a great gale of wind around his body. Pressure pushes out from his form, blowing Horokaida and I back a few steps as the demon continues to speak with controlled rage, "*All this time I've only wanted to see what happened to make you so broken. I wanted to SAVOR that moment, Brock, and you denied me that opportunity. You transgressed against one of the greatest ukjejido demons to have ever lived! GIVE ME WHAT I ASKED FOR!*"

Ekikon erupts with a blast of wind directed at both of us. The barrage he projects hits me like a heatwave, and, behind it, Ekikon screams one more time: "*YOU'RE A FAILURE, BROCK!*"

A metal block in the shape of a cylinder smashes into the top of Ekikon's skull.

A burst of grey light emits from the small metal pillar, which is etched with violet-colored runes all around it, and the weight of the cylinder cracks open the demon's skull, forcing out a jet of white blood which sputters all over its body.

"*You WRETCHES!*" Ekikon cries as tides of red and white mix into the shade of pale ruby and blast outward. "*Humans and their petty tricks—*"

The rune-covered cylinder is suddenly withdrawn and swung through the air while attached to a long chain. A much taller being who lurks behind Ekikon twirls the pillar and then slams it down upon the demon's head again; this time, its skull splinters and parts down the middle, and Ekikon's face dissolves into a violent wind filled with raining white blood.

I hear Ekikon's scream reverberate throughout the chamber, and, with that scream, I remember something I did as a teenager. A moment flashes before my eyes, one I don't want to see, and then it's gone.

In the place of Ekikon's dissolving body, another monster steps into view:

I see an abnormally long head that's flat at the top and extends out into two sharp points on its left and right. Green, beady eyes shine like haunting lights from a protruding face with slits for nostrils and a thin line with sharp teeth jutting out from it for a mouth. It towers over us with broad shoulders and a muscular, human-like body with ivy-colored fins attached to its hands and feet. Along its ribs, and in between a form covered in pale white skin, there are gills with sockets shaded in a deep grey; from those sockets, steam is emitted into a faint white cloud around its head, and this cloud matches the gleaming teeth it bares at us as it starts to speak in a deep, echoing tone.

"What toys do I have to play with today? Hmm."

Tyrick extends his spear and thrusts it toward the creature's head; in response, the pale Ajalu grabs the spear with one hand and swings its miniature pillar with the other. Tyrick ducks to avoid the attack, then he tries to free his weapon from his target's grasp. When the spear doesn't budge, I react before it can and toss the only grenade I have at the monster's feet.

The grenade bursts just as Ein throws one of her own. After two consecutive blasts, the pale Ajalu remains standing and uninjured. It twists the spear in its grasp and breaks the shaft in two.

Horokaida plunges into its field of vision, and he swings just as the Ajalu moves to block him with a swing of its own. When Horokaida's hammer connects with the metal pillar, a purple spark precedes a hard clang, and, following the sound of two powerful weapons smashing together, the Ajalu's runes come to life with violet light before slicing through metal; the chained pillar cuts the head of Horokaida's hammer in half, and Horokaida stumbles forward while still trying to complete his swing. With one end now halved and curved into a point, Horokaida lunges and stabs the Ajalu's abdomen: jagged metal cuts into a plane of hard flesh but doesn't pass through. As Horokaida's advance is halted by the thick skin of the pale beast, dark green blood flows from a shallow cut made within its stomach.

The Ajalu scowls, baring hundreds of needle-like teeth, and—

—SHUNGEJ—

Horokaida expands his arms and legs, lunges to the side of his opponent, and smashes in its right leg.

The Ajalu cries out with a deep bellow, appearing to slouch over for a moment. In that moment, I fire pistol rounds into its head while Ein reloads her sniper rifle and takes aim. My bullets bounce off my target's head like pebbles being shot into the cliffs of a mountain. Ein fires a round which rebounds off the creature's head without producing any reaction at all.

The pale Ajalu reels its head back, and, just as it snarls, it straightens its right leg back into place and begins flexing it before smiling back at us with teeth so sharp that they puncture the skin around its lips.

"Humans are my favorite prey. So violent, so passionate, so... fragile."

Syra rushes the Ajalu with a flaming sword, gripping it with both hands before she lunges into a powerful thrust aimed at the wound on its stomach. Just as the blade makes contact, with fire flickering around her opponent's lower body, the

Ajalu flashes out of reach and moves faster than any of us can anticipate. With a rapid spin, it throws its metal cylinder at Ein, who strafes to the right and moves within range to place another grenade within its open wound.

Ein rushes past the Ajalu, and the grenade explodes behind her. The impact blasts open shreds of skin to expose grey and white organs, and the white beast snarls as it twirls its weapon in the air while aiming once more at Ein's head.

I fire two more rounds into the left eye of the monster, but it doesn't react. Tyrick follows up by extending what's left of his spear into what looks like its liver, but the Ajalu pushes its palm against the end of the weapon and knocks it from Tyrick's grasp.

"We can't win!" he screams and sprints past the Ajalu.

"Stop giving up, you coward!" Syra shouts after him while readying her blade for another strike.

As Syra steps forward, something creeps up behind her.

A face with skin like ink and hair like midnight appears at Syra's side with glowing white eyes hovering above a toothless, ghost-white smile. The strange figure slouches over with its lanky body and grins while grabbing one of her arms. With her shoulder gash from earlier still exposed, it pulls at her arm with one hand and thrusts a long dagger into her muscle tissue.

"Help! Help me!" she screams.

Before any of us can reach her, the newcomer stabs at the wound again and again, deeper and deeper each time it cuts. After four quick thrusts, it tears Syra open on one side, then it proceeds to stab at the rest of her as she falls to the floor while it screeches with giddiness.

Ein reacts without showing emotion: she quickly retrieves Syra's blade, throws it to me, then she shouts, "Go!"

As we start to run past the pale Ajalu, Ein raises her rifle and fires a round into its left eye, piercing it and causing bright green blood to spill across its face.

Horokaida, Tyrick, Ein, and I sprint as a unit past enemies we have no hope of destroying. While we move underneath the watchful eyes of the giant meditating Ajalu, its head begins to turn; its smile disappears and is replaced by a grim scowl. When I refuse to look at it directly, it comes to me.

Like the demon before, this Ajalu burrows its way into my mind, and, even without staring into its empty eye sockets, I can see the image of its face digging into my mind, digging in and staring back at me. Its scowl turns into a smile once again, and it says, "**I know what you did, human. It happened when you were sixteen. Show me. Show me again and again.**"

Whereas the demon from before had to force my memories out of me, the sage merely says the words and I can't stop them from flowing through my mind.

I can't stop them, and so I remember someone else. Someone without a face, without a name...

--

In a vision where everything around me is black, I can remember being attacked by someone in a secluded room. I can remember being hit so hard that I fell to the floor and couldn't bear to stand.

I was still a teenager, and someone a few years older than me appeared from behind and grabbed the back of my neck. They forced my face into the ground and took off my belt before pulling down my pants.

With pain keeping me locked in place and fear holding me up within a daze, someone else kept me down and punched me in the head if I tried to move. They started to take my body without my permission, and...

--

"**And what?**" it asks as my squad races toward the next red door that's just come into view.

"Don't make me remember," I tell it. "I don't want to remember."

"**Your resistance is so powerful for an untrained human. If you remember this, you'll remember what happened in that room with all those soldiers, won't you?**"

I repeat, "I don't want to remember."

"But you will."

--

A stranger took advantage of my body without my permission. When I asked them to stop, when I tried to get up, he kept punching me. Punching and punching, calling me his and putting himself inside me.

He punched me one more time, and then I stood up. All my pain melted away.

I elbowed him in the face, then I punched him in his right temple. He passed out, but I kept hitting him. Without remembering his face, I climbed atop this stranger's body and punched and punched, just like he did. My fists bashed in his nose, crushed his eye sockets inward, shattered his jaw into fragments. I punched and punched, splattering blood across the ground and getting my fists wet in a pit of catharsis.

I never wanted anyone's body for myself, but, when my body was taken from me, all I wanted was to smash the form of the perpetrator, to break it into nothing. I wanted to smash that demon's head until there was nothing left.

--

"And there he is. Right there inside of you. I've been waiting for him to appear."

We make it to the next door, and it's already unlocked. Horokaida leads us into the next room, a room with scarlet red tiles instead of white and much smaller than any chamber we've passed through before. The next door is right in front of us. Tyrick and Ein remove their gas masks, and Horokaida speaks for the whole group.

"I'm proud of everyone for having made it this far," he says while the light of his aura begins to grow around him. "When we make it through this, we'll be recognized for everything that we did."

"How can you say that when I don't even have a weapon?" Tyrick exclaims, "How am I supposed to defend mys—"

Ein cuts him off by handing him her pistol. "Shut up and move," she says. "While you've been whining, I've been having a lot of fun."

"You're crazy!" Tyrick takes the gun from her and says as his eyes widen.

Horokaida slaps him in the head, then he points toward the metal latch on the next door, "Let's hurry. We got a short break, but it's not over."

I hear the groaning call of the giant Ajalu behind us as we pass through the next door and into a narrow room which veers off to the left and forms a hallway carpeted with purple velvet. An exposed lightbulb hangs down by a wire from the hallway ceiling, and the walls are all a pallid white.

Horokaida takes position at the front-right of a new formation; I move down the hallway with him on the left and keep my eyes fixed on the sights of my pistol as I move forward. Tyrick and Ein walk with their backs to ours as they watch out for our rear flank.

With security established in both directions, we proceed down the hallway and past the illumination of the lightbulb into the gloom of a dark corridor. We reach the corner at its end, and Horokaida stops a couple feet back before gesturing for me to begin pieing off the blind spot ahead. I sidestep around the corner while staying far back and maintain a forward-leaning stance as I focus my eyes down the barrel of the pistol.

I see another dark corridor which stretches on until meeting the next red door not far ahead. When I see that the way is clear, Horokaida and I change positions: I move to the front-right and he to the front-left; Tyrick and Ein don't switch, but Ein begins moving closer to our backs while putting a short distance between her and Tyrick. Tyrick becomes the foremost element of our rearguard, with Ein staying behind him because she's got the better weapon.

We move through darkness, with our only light being the scarlet shine coming through the cracks within the next doorframe. While our approach speeds up, I feel Ein halt behind me.

"Stop," she says.

Horokaida turns and puts his back to the wall so that he can look both ways with a quick glance. I turn completely and look down the hallway behind us to see a dark puddle forming at its center. Black liquid spreads with bubbles that rise to the surface before flying toward the ceiling.

I hear the sound of an explosion at my back, an eruption which screeches and shakes the whole room. While all of us turn toward the door, Horokaida keeps his eyes fixed behind me and points firmly as he says, "Don't look away!"

When I look back down the corridor, the hulking, pale body of the Ajalu from earlier appears above the puddle and steps through dark liquid to look down at Tyrick. Tyrick freezes in shock and shakes while peering up to meet the pale beast's gaze.

The Ajalu points one clawed finger at Tyrick's pistol and says to him, **"Here's what we're going to do, little human. You're going to point the gun at me and tell me that you're the hero. You're going to say that I am the villain, that I can be defeated.**

"You'll attack me, and I'll let you try to be the hero that you want to be. When you're finished, I'll show you the end of the play. Are you ready? Attack me."

Tyrick shoots the Ajalu in the face. His bullet rebounds off its forehead, so he fires another round into its bleeding eye socket, and this one also rebounds and nearly hits him. Behind Tyrick, Ein fires a round from her sniper rifle into the eye that's still intact—

The Ajalu catches it with one hand and throws it back at her. Ein ducks, and Tyrick panics and begins shooting it in the head over and over again. Each bullet barely manages to nudge the creature's body, and so it begins to walk toward us while calmly ignoring its attackers. Ein fires another round, reloads, and then another, but the pale beast merely grabs her bullets out of the air and tosses them back in our direction.

Acting as the wisest among us, Horokaida smacks my right shoulder with his hand, shouts, "Let's go," and sprints toward the next door. With a quick look back, I tap Ein's shoulder and gesture for her to do the same.

"Thank you, Tyrick," Ein says and fires one last shot that's caught by the Ajalu before running with the rest of us toward the door.

On our way out, I look back to catch a final glimpse of Tyrick's struggle for survival. "Wait!" he screams while taking a moment to watch us leave. When he sees us departing, he sighs and fires the last round within his magazine. Tyrick draws a knife and shouts, "You're the villain! You can be defeated!"

Tyrick rushes to stab the Ajalu in the chest; it swipes with one hand and tears Tyrick's face from his skull. As blood spurts from the hole left behind and Tyrick's body hits the floor, I turn to enter the next room.

Rather than a hallway, we walk into a small chamber like the one before it, and, as soon as we do, we're surrounded.

An Ajalu with greying skin and the body of an undead human corpse rushes at Horokaida and buries a knife into the top of his bicep!

—**SHUNGEJ**—

Horokaida expands the same bicep and punches the Ajalu. He blasts its head open with one strike, then he swings his fist to the side and blasts open the head of the second incoming beast. A third approaches, and Horokaida uppercuts it so fiercely that he drives his fist through its stomach.

A large black puddle forms at the other side of the room. From this puddle, dozens of shriveled bodies emerge before the image of the meditating sage appears once again. The sage Ajalu shrinks down to my size and beams its smile my way while droves of ravenous creatures fall upon us.

Horokaida and I stand in front of Ein, and, while he tightens a two-handed grip around his hammer, I reload my pistol and begin firing upon an incoming wave of shriveled creatures.

As we protect Ein, she takes a shot at the sage, and, in response, an oval shield the color of amethyst suddenly appears and surrounds it to block the bullet.

"Dammit," she says under her breath before reloading and focusing her fire on the beasts attacking me.

To my left, Horokaida channels zol into his arms and starts to swing with rapid speed mixed with incredible strength; each swing connects with multiple opponents at once and knocks them back while smashing their bodies open in the process. To conserve ammo, I start to swing with the heatblade left behind by Syra, and, with each stroke, I cut through torsos, arms, legs, and necks. I generate so much heat that my hands begin to burn from a sword that echoes out flames in a growing arc.

"**Very good,**" says the sage at the other end of the room. "**That memory is just on the surface of your thoughts, pulling them into it like a sinkhole which never stops.**"

It stretches out one decrepit hand and sends forth a flow of black energy that wraps around the bodies of four of the sprawling undead.

"**Let me make things a little harder for you, human. Together, you'll stand. Together, you'll bleed.**"

Four bodies stitch themselves into a bigger creation, with broad, grey bones wrapped in writhing strands of thick flesh. A head made of dark tendrils forms around a rotting white skull, and a skinny behemoth slouches forward while it prepares to charge our way. A burst of dark light flows behind it, and the behemoth runs toward Horokaida.

Horokaida, reacting on instinct, charges as well and lowers his broken hammer to his waist as he roars, "Brock, attack on the right!"

The beast swings at Horokaida's head, he crouches low and ducks, and then he smashes his hammer into its abdomen. The netite hammer produces a loud "thud" along with firing a rain of blue sparks as it connects and forces a strong vibration throughout the behemoth's body. Instead of causing any visible damage, Horokaida's attack stops the charge of the beast;

in response, it grabs at his head. From the right, I swing and sever its arm before it can reach him, then I swing down and sever its right leg out from under it.

The behemoth falls on its face, then it quickly rolls back and forth on the ground and swings out to strike Horokaida as it cuts three deep gashes into his cheek. Horokaida responds by crushing its head with his hammer.

"Help!" we both turn as we hear Ein's voice.

Just as Ein blows off the head of one Ajalu, five more begin to swarm her. Behind them, yet another behemoth begins to form from a collection of six decaying bodies.

"Does it feel familiar?" I hear the sage ask.

Horokaida and I rush to Ein's defense; I slice off the head of one enemy, and Horokaida bashes in the head of another; I rend through the sunken ribcages of two, and Horokaida swings with enough force to blast back three.

Ein recovers by firing a round into the head of the incoming behemoth, but it charges through to swing at me. I see its hand fly before my face, and I run my blade through its palm. I arc my sword outward, cut its hand in two, then I thrust down through the bone of its right kneecap. When it lurches forward from the pain, Horokaida steps in and swings overhead: he bashes in the beast's skull, which causes dark blood to spray over my face.

I rush under the legs of one slain creature and into the arms of another. A third behemoth reaches for me with both hands, and Horokaida bashes in the side of one of its arms; when it continues to reach with its right, Ein shoots its right shoulder blade into fragments, and I lunge to shove my flaming sword through its skull.

But it doesn't work.

The beast grabs at my left side and sinks its claws deep into my skin. I swing down and out, decapitate it, and Horokaida rips its arm away just as six smaller beasts begin to swarm us.

At our backs, another behemoth rushes at Ein on all fours, like a dark leopard running toward its prey. Ein shoots it in the head, yet it continues to move forward until its upon her before we can react.

Ein screams, and I sprint to her defense. The leopard Ajalu bares fangs at its next meal. Its head lunges for hers, and I launch myself forward while thrusting out; I stab it in the head just as its teeth almost pierce Ein's eye, then, while on my knee, I stab and stab at its body, ripping hole after hole and tearing through its flesh while Ein scrambles to get to her feet.

"Brock, watch your right!" Horokaida shouts.

To my right, the biggest behemoth I've encountered, standing at over fifteen feet tall and hulking with the size of eight undead corpses piled together, hurdles my way and with one claw extended behind it. The giant moves rapidly and swings with a razor-sharp claw attached to thickened, grey muscle.

Horokaida plunges his hammer downward, connecting the head of it with the beast's arm, and smashes it into the ground!

With its left, the beast thrusts its remaining claw through Horokaida's chest. Yellowed blades plunge through skin and bone, and the collection of flesh and grey tissue tears into Horokaida and emerges from outside of his upper back, spraying blood in its wake.

The great behemoth holds the broken body of my comrade high in the air, and Horokaida screams, "Brock! Take the last of my energy! Awaken, Brock. Awaken and protect Ein!"

At once, Horokaida cries out with an explosion of solid white aura. His aura projects in a massive halo around his body while giving off a radiant light; this light causes every being but the sage to reel back and emit a screech that ricochets off each wall and causes my ears to ring. Wisps of light draw toward me, open the pores in my skin, and fill my body with energy which demands to be unleashed. I clench one fist and feel pressure build within my whole arm; I tighten my grip on my sword, and that same pressure bolsters the fire around it; it makes me indifferent to the scorching flames as they gather around my hand.

Before my eyes, the behemoth screams with rage and slams Horokaida's body down upon the ground. It slams him so hard that the back of his head breaks open and I hear the sound of his bones being crushed against the strength of the impact from its throw.

Without thinking, I race toward the behemoth and feel tremendous power move down into my legs. I jump from the floor onto the top of its forearm, jump from its forearm toward its one-eyed head, and slice its face in two. My momentum carries me forward enough that I can land on its shoulder, and, from there, I swing again and sever its head from its shoulders. As dark blood wells from the stump left behind, the beast reaches for me with both claws; I leap from its shoulder onto the ground, and the great behemoth twitches before falling to the floor.

Just when I land, I see Ein being swarmed once again by five more of the bastards. When I try to run toward her, an Ajalu on my right slices into my shoulder with its claw. On my left, another tears into my left cheek. I punch one in the head and decapitate the other. I move forward again, but I'm tackled from the side. I almost fall over but regain my footing as power continues to cause my body to shake. I elbow the Ajalu who tackled me in the face, pushing it backward, and then two more sink their claws into my back as I watch Ein drop her sniper rifle.

"It's almost over for you. Don't you want to remember one last time? Remember what you did, human?"

I pull myself free and keep moving toward her, but yet another of the devils stands in my way. I thrust my bleeding shoulder into its chest; it absorbs the blow and grabs me in its embrace, sinking its claws into my back. I push one of its arms out, and it reacts by biting into my right trapezius muscle. An Ajalu from behind catches up with me and grabs at the head of the bunny hanging out of the pouch attached to my waist. I punch it in the head hard enough to bury my knuckles into its skull, and it falls forward before turning around and rushing me again. I punch through the neck of the devil biting into my trapezius, kick it to the ground, and, all at once, three of the Ajalu grab me: one on the left, one in front, and one behind.

I'm held in place and watch as Ein shoots with her pistol and stabs at each Ajalu that tries to swarm her. As four try to tackle her at once, she cuts at their necks and shoots one of them in the head while a behemoth begins to form a short distance behind her.

"Brock," she screams when one of them tears out a chunk in her neck, "help me!"

"Hurry up," she shouts again as another sinks its claws into her chest.

I try to move, but now five of them have me within their grasps, have me completely surrounded. While I fight my way forward, I'm forced to watch as one of the Ajalu around Ein grabs her face with its hand; another of the Ajalu holding me back reaches for the bunny again.

"Go ahead," I hear the sage speak to me, **"remember."**

--

I'm in a room with over a dozen other soldiers. I can't see their faces, and I can't see their ranks. I remember expressions: hate and desire all meeting in the middle and where one of them taunts me; he asks me over and over again about Ronas.

"It was your fault," he says. "You could've stopped us and you didn't. You could've stopped us, but you chose to be a coward—"

"You're just a coward," the sage's voice mixes with his—

"Just a coward," the soldier repeats. "You let us do it to him. That makes you nothing. It makes you too weak, too stupid, and that means that you might as well have done it yourself. That's right, *you* did it. It's not true, sure, but that's what we'll tell the rest of the battalion—"

"It's your fault—"

"We're going to do to you what we did to him, and you're going to fucking like it, you understand? You'll like it, and, at the end, we'll break your bones. We're going to break you down, Brock—"

"It's your fault—"

"We'll break you, then we'll tell everyone that you broke him. We'll tell them that, and then they'll shoot you, like the stupid bastard you are! Get him!"

One of them tries to grab me, and I deck him hard enough to make him fall to the ground. Another approaches too fast; he hits like a brick and busts my nose. When I try to return a strike of my own, he pushes my hand to the side and punches me in the cheekbone. A third guy kicks my side, and a fourth ambushes me from behind: he puts me in a headlock as the others begin shouting with excitement.

"Get him down on the ground!" one says.

"Keep hitting him," chimes in another.

I'm pushed to my knees by three men.

"It's your fault."

They grab my head and slam it against the ground. I lose teeth, and blood starts to pour out from my mouth.

I don't want to remember. I don't want to remember. Please stop.

--

One of the Ajalu keeps pulling at the stuffed animal when he's not supposed to. Ein struggles to break free as a claw digs into her face, and she grabs onto the arm of another devil to keep it from digging any farther. I feel that memory coming back, and it makes me weak. They rip and tear at my body, and all my energy goes toward protecting the one good memory I have left, toward protecting a small white bunny from a horde of beasts. I have to stay here, but I can't. I have to stay in the present, I have to protect Ein, but...

--

I'm stuck in that memory. Those men push me to the ground, and I hear the sound of belts being unbuckled.

"All right, boys," I hear their ringleader speak, "looks like we've pinned down this one without problem. Remember: he killed Ronas. He's a piece of shit. Make him pay for it."

One of them grabs at my belt—

"It's all your fault."

One hits me across the back of my head with the buttstock of his rile—

"It's all your fault."

They take off my pants, one of them tries to put himself inside of me, and…

He wakes up.

The room becomes red with their blood.

--

When I look at Ein again, I feel all the hope drain out of me.

The Ajalu grabbing her digs one claw into her eye. It digs and tears outward, breaking bone and spraying blood out of the right side of her face. "BROCK," she screams and falls to her knees as they throw themselves upon her.

Another Ajalu grabs at the stuffed animal at my waist at the same time that I do. I try to save it, to save Alina, but I can't.

It rips it away. It tears off its head.

Alina's smile fades into nothing, and then I hear it one last time:

"It's all your fault."

--

The Guardian

--

I am awake.

10
Disassociation

--

The Guardian

--

WHEN I AWAKEN, I can't stop laughing.

I laugh, and then I put my fist through the first skull I see. I punch through grey flesh, sending up a waterfall of black, then I strike with the side of my fist and blast through the head of the next bastard. I break apart the skull of a third with another punch, then I punch again, elbow, and ram my straightened palm through the head of another abomination.

I see Ein being torn into, and I sprint. It takes less than a second to reach her, less than a second to grab two necks and break them, and less than a second to ram my knee through the head of the Ajalu on top of her.

I hear screaming in my head. I see blood. I feel rage like hot wrath.

I kick out and drive my foot through one head, then I kick forward and burst open another. I spin and crash my knee through the face of a third bastard, then I laugh, grab the neck of another, and start to punch and punch. When others begin to swarm me, I grab Ein's pistol and shoot one in the head. I burst open the skulls of two more with two quick punches, then I drive my elbow through the entire chest of yet another stupid Ajalu scum.

I shoot, then I punch. I grab Ein's knife, then I start stabbing, cutting open throats, slicing through eye sockets, and jamming the blade into chests and stomachs. I tear through skin and shoot as they continue to approach.

Ein reaches up at me from the ground with only one eye. I take her hand in one of mine and shoot an incoming behemoth. When it gets too close, I rush toward it, jump, and drive my heel through its kneecap; at the same time, I shoot up and through its skull, then I put my fist through its stomach to send black blood jetting out from the other side. From within, I feel jagged bone cut open my arm, so I pull back and rush back toward Ein as the behemoth falls to the ground behind me.

While three more Ajalu reach toward Ein, I run at the first and stab it in the side of its head; I run at the second, rotate my body on one leg, and kick its ugly face from its shoulders; I turn to face the third and fire three rounds—one to the stomach, one to the chest, and one through its right eye. As a few more move my way, I punch their heads open and fire upon another swarm before it can outflank me.

Ein reaches up again. This time, she makes eye contact with me and whispers, "Who are you?"

I feel adrenaline build within my veins and cause my body to quake. My thoughts race in line with the speed of my pulse, and then a light the color of a sapphire jewel emerges from around my hands and arms. I feel my mind become clear while a tidal wave rises within me.

Blue becomes pale blue, pulsating with strength which ripples out and causes the muscles in my body to tense and move of their own accord. Another wave, then another. Power like no other builds and builds until…

Until aura spills out all around me. Ein grows pale as she watches my confidence start to build within a hopeless place. I start to laugh again, and I finally answer her question.

"I'm here to protect *him*. To protect the both of you. I'll kill all of them, Ein. I'll smash apart every single one of them."

Just as another behemoth approaches, I spring from my feet with a powerful leap and drive the front of my elbow into its skull. I kick out and smash through the rest of its face and then descend to punch through two more Ajalu heads before I turn to face the sage.

The sage grins back at me.

"That's what I wanted to see. Now, let me test your resolve."

The grinning Ajalu dissolves but leaves behind the figure of Kalina, who holds a spear out to her side and smiles as she says to me, "It's mine. I'll take it again, and, if you don't let me,"—she extends the point of the spear my way—"I'll kill you, Brock honey."

Without hesitation, she flashes toward me with a wicked laugh. I sense and feel the wind behind her movements, dodge her spear with a sidestep, and punch toward her head.

My fist meets air, and her form disappears as the sage's laugh echoes throughout the room. The red door across from me swings open, and it beckons me forward:

"Come on," it says, **"show me how you did it. Show me what you did to them."**

I step through the door and into the next chamber. In this room, I see all the faces from that memory, and I see all the same expressions as before. A squad of soldiers looks at me all at once. They grin at the same time, then they rush at me in a column.

I see the blackened face of the first soldier; I send a haymaker his way and, with it, his head. I uppercut the second soldier, forcing my fist through his gut, then I slam him into the one behind him. I draw my knife, and I cut the throat of the fourth, jab a fifth three times in the stomach, slash open the face of the sixth, and shoot the seventh in the head.

Several more emerge from small black puddles scattered throughout the room. I move toward the center as the chamber's walls and floors become scarlet red. I feel power, a bloodlust beyond which I've ever felt before.

"Show me. Show me what you did to them."

I slash and stab, kick and punch; I throw my body to the left and thrust my elbow through the nose and face of one enemy; I place my hand around his shoulder, and use this as leverage to swing around his body and kick off the head of another opponent. I land on both feet, then I shoot with a two-handed grip as I back away. I shoot three Ajalu soldiers through their skulls, and, when I run out of ammo, I throw my pistol against the head of another.

They surround me, and I cut my way through them. They grab at my clothes, and I kick in their kneecaps before ramming my fists through their skulls, one by one.

The next door opens, and I run through. There's more red on the other side, and the door slams behind me.

"Come on!" I yell before starting to laugh again, "Bring me more! MORE!"

It becomes quiet. I hear the voice of Kalina screaming in my head, cursing me for destroying her image, cursing me for not giving up my body again. My memories of her cause me to clench my fists, and my memories of the room, the room where I spilled so much blood, fill my body with a scorching heat. I have to unleash this. I have to.

In front, a black puddle appears and begins to spread. From this puddle, what looks like the top of a hammerhead shark floats to the surface; as it begins to rise, I see the smiling face of the pale Ajalu who I thought I'd left behind me.

While we make eye contact, it swings its rune-covered pillar through the air and says, "**Little human—**"

But I cut him off, stagger my stance as I raise my fists, and tell him, "Here's what we're going to do. I'll play the villain and you play the hero. You're going to call me "little" again, then you're going to try to hit me with that bitchly thing you call a weapon. You're going to think that you're strong enough to crush me, and I'm going to let you think that.

"And then, like the filthy demon you are, I'll break your neck."

Its expression becomes blank, staring at me as though I'm stupid. It begins again, "**Little human—**"

And I rush toward it with fire burning in my veins.

The pale beast swings its pillar at my head, I slide under its attack, then I lift my body upward with my momentum; the Ajalu reaches for me with its other hand, but I focus my speed into a downward elbow thrust and ram my elbow into its upper thigh. I strike, and the force of my attack causes the Ajalu to grunt before it reaches for me a second time. I swing my body to the left while using its upper thigh as a pivot point, then I rotate myself around the Ajalu, punch it in the back, and try to kick in the back of one of its knees.

It doesn't work. The Ajalu kicks out behind itself, and I'm forced to sidestep. It moves so that its side is facing me, then it kicks; I duck under its leg, run toward the other as it grabs for me, and move to the left, out of reach, before I punch the side of its kneecap and run forward when it still doesn't budge. As I try to flee, it swings its metal weapon and strikes the back of my head. I fall forward and almost onto my face but catch myself with my hands. In spite of the beast's tremendous strength, its weapon barely left a mark. Nothing will break The Guardian.

I manage to stand quickly, but the Ajalu moves faster. It zooms before my eyes to appear in front of me with the same smile as before.

"**Go ahead,**" it says, "**give me that speech again.**"

I smile back, chuckle, and tell him, "You're a joke. You're too weak to fight m—"

It soars to meet me before I can move and reaches for my face with an open claw. When I throw my body to the right, barely avoiding its grasp, it swings and dashes me across the head with its pillar, but I've become too tough for it to bring me down.

I turn to face it, still standing, and it says to me, "**Interesting. That strike should've been enough to cave in your skull, little human. Let me give it another try.**"

I run toward it with a closed fist; it meets me head on, swings, and smashes its weapon against my face, busting open the bridge of my nose.

I punch out at its head; it zooms around me to smack its pillar against my back and nearly push me off my feet.

I turn around to face the Ajalu; it races by me, then it smashes the pillar against the side of my head. It swings again and smacks my ribcage, and then, growing frustrated, it grabs at my face with its open claw once more.

When I duck, it turns and smashes the pillar against the top of my head hard enough to cause my vision to blur.

I black out.

--

I open my eyes, and I'm standing on the upper deck of a massive, grey aircraft sailing high above an open desert. I look over the railing with a familiar face, and he smiles back at me.

Horokaida looks me over and says, "This isn't you. Where's Brock? Who's the person standing in front of me right now?"

"It doesn't matter," I tell him. "I've come to protect Brock. I was defeated."

"Hmph," he smirks and says, "No. You weren't defeated. I pulled you out in time in order to explain some things. But I can see in your eyes that this isn't 'Brock' that I'm speaking to. Who are you?"

"As I said, I'm protecting him. I'm protecting him because no one else will. His mother tried to save him, and she couldn't do it. When Brock was left in the dark to die, when those men tried to hurt him, I took over. I've taken over again, and I'm going to destroy every predator that's still alive. I'll smash them. I'll break them. I am The Guardian."

"I see," Horokaida continues smirking and looks down as he replies, "you sound more confident than before. I think I like this side of you a little better. Do you still remember who I am, Guardian?"

I breathe in deeply as I clench my fists. "I do. I couldn't save you, and I failed. I have to avenge you, Horokaida."

"Slow down there, buddy." Horokaida chuckles, "You just might do it. When I prayed with you, I made the choice to leave behind an image that would help you where you need it the most. This is the last time you'll see me, Bro—I mean, 'The Guardian.'"

Horokaida takes his Maia Handbook out from a pouch around his waist and flips the book open to a page I can't see.

"I have to send you back, but my spirit will be going with you. If you're Brock's guardian, then I'm going to need you to channel your aura when I tell you to. You're going to focus it on the weapon you need the most, the weapon you need more than anything else. Take all the energy you can and concentrate it into what you think you'll need to survive. If you make it count, then you can save him. Got it?"

"Yeah," I tell him as I feel adrenaline surge through my veins again, "I can do it. I can kill that thing."

--

My vision goes dark, and then I can see again in the present world.

I feel as though I'm drenched with sweat as I open my eyes to see a room of red all around me. I blink, then I see the image of the pale Ajalu standing in front of me. It swings its metal pillar with a grin and says, "**There you are. You stood still like a little human statue. I watched you to see if you'd die standing. I'm impressed by your durability.**"

I look back at him and feel the aura of Horokaida close by. In my mind, I hear his voice, "*Picture it. I'll give you the rest of the power I have, and then I'll have to go. When I leave, it'll be up to you. Picture it, and I'll give you enough power to chant. Save him. Save Ein, too.*"

I stand tall. I have no feeling other than pure resolve, than the pure intent to overcome a powerful enemy.

The Ajalu staggers its stance and raises one claw as it swings its pillar in the shape of a helix. It says to me, "**Here's what we're going to do. You're going to play the hero and I'm going to play the villain. You'll start to think that you're winning, and I'll let you think that, then I'll rip off both of your arms and shove them into your mouth.**

"**The human race is a stepping stone. The demon race is but a nuisance. Demons chase their urges into oblivion, using their power for nothing but self-gratification. Humans struggle to 'be,' to 'become,' to define meaning through how they exist; they are too weak to thrive or to grow. Your heroism is entirely wasted, for humans will soon make way for the Ajalu.**

"The Mulungus calls for a higher form of being. It feasts on the agony of human weakness and derives from it a greater evolution which is more deserving of this earthly plane than your kin. Because of your pain, your fear, and your depravity, we thrive. For centuries, very few of us could speak. Now, I, Ixilho, the harbinger, will communicate to you how you'll die, little fledgling.

"I will be the villain," it says again, **"and I will put an end to humanity. Right here."**

"Now," I hear Horokaida, *"hurry up and do it now!"*

Ixilho zooms toward me, but my eyes have adjusted to his speed.

I dash to the side, turn, and—

—**MAIA: GENESIS**—

A barrel of shining blue metal forms out of bright, blooming particles gathering between both of my arms. While a broad hunk of metal rests over one hand, a handle and trigger begin to form in the other. A line of zol is drawn from my right eye to blue, translucent sights which enhance my eyesight when I look through them. In both hands, I now carry a cerulean machine gun. I aim it at the pale beast and start to spray.

Instead of lead, bullets of zol burst into the Ajalu's body like small spears containing frenetic energy. This frenetic energy strikes his skin hard enough to almost pierce it, and, instead of rebounding, each bullet explodes to the chagrin of Ixilho. As sapphire-colored lights rain over him, I hear Ixilho snarl before he dashes toward me and lunges to swing downward.

I roll to the side, Ixilho smashes his pillar into the ground next to me, then he reaches toward me with his other hand.

"Flip the weapon; use the other side," Horokaida's voice rings through my head.

I duck under Ixilho's claw as it flashes by, spin my machine gun so that its buttstock faces toward him, and the buttstock expands into a large hunk of metal.

I use it like a bat. I swing and smash it against Ixilho's thigh, and his thigh breaks inward as it gushes with green blood.

Ixilho cries out and swings his pillar at my head, but I draw back, slide across the floor, flip my weapon again, and fire a barrage of rounds into his head. While the rest of my bullets cause his head to rock back, one of them pierces his other eye, leading to two eye sockets that drain green liquid across his face.

Ixilho pivots on one foot, and then, using his one working leg, he springs at me while waving his weapon overhead. Ixilho slashes down with the pillar, and I throw the full length of my machine gun up to block his attack; metal rings against metal, and his strike causes me to stagger backward while maintaining the integrity of the zol gun. Ixilho falls forward with a harsh scream, and I bury a dozen rounds into his skull and shoulders. This time, my rounds create small cuts in his skin and cause his bones to crack.

Ixilho looks up at me and shouts, **"Play your role, little human! This is the stage of your demise! DIE ON THE STAGE!"**

Ixilho drops his weapon and jumps at me!

Rather than back away, I feel something within urging me forward. I feel confidence bolstered by the presence of another force. The pale Ajalu reaches for me with open claws, I rush toward him, and—

—SHUNGEJ—

The spirit of Horokaida appears above me and with a hammer in both hands. He lifts his hammer high, then he brings it down across Ixilho's head, slamming the beast into the ground while giving me the chance to press the barrel of my gun into the Ajalu's skull.

I hear Horokaida one last time.

"Finish him. Focus your aura around one bullet and end him. This is my final bit of advice to you: destroy the enemy; don't give up and save everyone you can. Goodbye, Brock."

Just as he orders, I wait to fire, channeling everything I have into a light which glows near the trigger well before moving down along the barrel. This light expands into a radiant burst of energy, and it builds while remaining at the exit point at the end of the metal shaft.

Ixilho wearily looks up at me again, through the streams of green blood running down his face, and he says to me, "**Feeble human, you've taken hold of a power that you don't deserve. Your aura is a toxic stain upon this world, so says the Mulungus. It speaks to us, its myriad of creations, and tells us what your kind has done.**

"**Your kind has grown despicably, as if you were insulting what created you from the beginning. As you were not meant to grow beyond your beginnings, this growth has brought about a plague of your own making. Regardless of how much you fight, the Ajalu, the first evolution of the Mulungus' spawn, will surpass you. We will consume all life that dwells upon this world and make it our own. Yes,**" it speaks with maddened glee, "**we will reform the world in our image. We will become the prime organisms of this realm and through a plague which never ends.**"

"Here's what we're going to do then," I tell him, "I'll be the batter and you'll be the pitcher. What does the batter say to the pitcher?"

"**Little hu—**"

I spin my machine gun around to its extended buttstock, then I slam the hunk of metal down onto its head as I shout, "Catch this!"

Ixilho's skull caves under the impact, and the pale Ajalu's head is smashed into a pool of bones and green blood.

11
The Last Chamber

--

The Guardian

--

I CROSS ONE ROOM AND PASS THROUGH AN-
OTHER. Walls and floors of dark red turn to pale white,
and each following chamber echoes with the sound of my
footsteps as I continue passing through pale, open doors.

My body grows tired after moving through what feels like
thirty or so empty chambers. I no longer know, as each one
begins to blur together. When I finally slow down after passing
through yet another door, I hear the voice of the meditating
Ajalu ring throughout the empty rooms around me:

**"So much of your life has been wasted serving others.
Why do you think The Guardian appeared?"**

"Because no one else would protect him," I say back. "You
know this already."

The lights emitted by the cubed, netite flooring flicker on
and off.

**"You chose to follow the guidance of others, to be-
come subservient. Brock had no mind of his own; he was
merely driven by the orders handed down to him. You became what he needed when orders no longer sufficed. For
his entire life, and from his conception as a child on the
battlefield, Brock has been guided by minds other than
his own. He never became a person. Rather, Brock became an object to be repurposed over and over again,
and,"**—the lights flicker once more—**"when that object sus-
tained too much trauma, it developed a second persona.
You are The Guardian, and I will submerge you in the
chaos from which you wish to escape."**

"How do you plan on doing that?"

The lights flicker a third time, and then a child appears before me. I see the face of Alina, and she stares back at me with
a worried look.

"**Go to your child. She's the only happy memory that's been left to you and Brock; she's a part of the reason why The Guardian exists, correct? You exist to protect the weak.**"

I run toward her, the lights go off, and then I reach Alina just as she disappears.

From behind, a creature attacks me.

A figure with two long knives and long, black hair thrusts one of its blades toward my back. I turn to avoid the strike, then I swing my machine gun around as fast as I can; the black-haired demon backsteps to evade me and then gazes at me with glowing white eyes and a dark, narrow smile.

The Ajalu who cut open and killed Syra laughs, then it darts to my left, runs toward me, and slashes at my head. I turn again, swinging the hunk of metal faster this time, but the Ajalu leaps up onto my weapon, jumps again to land behind me, and then it strikes!

It thrusts one blade into my back…

But its knife doesn't pierce me.

I turn for the final time, and, when it dodges, I light up the room with a spray of bullets made from my aura. As it tries to escape to the left, I move my aim ahead of it. I fire four glowing rounds of energy through its torso, shredding open its chest and stomach as its smile becomes an open-mouthed look of despair.

The last round I fire absorbs the whole of the machine gun into one great blast of sapphire-colored aura. My weapon becomes the round itself, and, once it makes contact with the body of the Ajalu, the round consumes it completely. My last attack causes its form to be burned away into almost nothing, leaving shreds of black behind in its wake.

At that same moment, Ein rushes through the door at my back and appears in the room behind me.

"Brock!" she screams while covering her bleeding eye socket with one hand. "How did you take them all out?"

When I see that she's still alive, it doesn't feel real. I don't sense any emotion coming from within me, but I'm glad that she made it this far.

"I don't really know how I did it," I tell her, and, as I try to answer her question...

I begin to fade.

--

Brock

--

I feel myself wake up from a long dream. I feel at ease, and then my nerves are bothering me again. Ein's right before my eyes, and she's looking at me like she's afraid of something.

"What's wrong?" I ask her.

"You... you changed," she says while still covering her eye. "Your mind went blank, didn't it? I saw you change just now."

"I didn't change," is my reply. "I'm still me."

She pauses while looking me over, and it's then that I notice small vibrations in the air around her body. I see short wavelengths that are tinted green, and, along her exposed arm and shoulder, I notice veins being pressed out from all over.

"Are you okay?" I ask her.

Ein looks down, shakes her head, and says, "No. What I saw from you wasn't normal, and *I* don't feel normal, either. I know that Horokaida died back there, and you changed, Brock. When you changed, it affected me, too, and now I can't stop feeling whatever it was that took you over."

Ein grabs both of my shoulders and looks into my eyes. "Brock, we have to get out of here. I don't want to fight them anymore."

"**Yes,**" I hear the voice of the Ajalu sage, "**come closer. Move to the end of the maze and I'll explain to you how your lives will end.**"

On cue, each door leading into the subsequent rooms ahead of us swings open. I see down the length of each chamber, all the way to the end of the tunnel. At the end, I see the dark form of the Ajalu sage in meditation. It reaches toward me and gestures for us to approach.

"**Come on,**" it says, "**the game has neared its end.**"

I start to walk forward with Ein, but she halts and says, "Wait," while looking into my eyes with fear.

"What's wrong?"

"That thing," she says, "has it been talking to you, too? I keep hearing its voice, but I'm not sure it's real. It keeps asking about my mom."

"It's real," I explain, "it's been digging through my history without my permission. It brought out the worst in me."

"No, it didn't. It just caused you to change is all. That thing knows about what my mom used to do to me, and, if it keeps bringing up that memory, I won't make it, Brock."

"C'mon," I nudge her while moving on, "I'll kill it for you, then we can get out of here."

Ein nervously follows behind me, and then she stops as soon as we pass through and into the next room. Ein puts her hand against the wall and tries to slow her breathing.

"Dammit," she says under her breath. Ein gathers herself, then she puts one foot forward and screams at the sage, "Fuck you! I remember it well enough—you don't have to make me go over it again! Dammit!"

"Ein," I ask while looking her over with concern, "what happened? That thing made me remember my daughter. Alina passed away a few years back, and I wasn't... I wasn't strong enough to keep her from dying."

"Heh," Ein chuckles.

"Why's that funny?"

Ein gives me a dark look and says, "I wasn't 'strong enough' to stop myself from killing her."

"Killing who?"

"My mom!" she screams as her face flushes red, "I killed her! I killed her, you stupid idiot! She let her asshole boyfriends molest me, and so I started killing them, one by one! Do you understand?"

"I do," I tell her quietly.

"Then get the fuck out of my face, Brock!" she shouts with rage. "GO!"

I walk away from her without another word.

As I proceed into the next room, I hear Ein's voice become louder. She shrieks with pain and begins to cry. When I look behind me, I see what was small vibrations before become emerald waves that ripple through the air around her. Ein develops an aura which radiates out from her with enough power to cause my adrenaline to spike again. I feel something within me reaching for my mind, reaching and trying to take it from me. But I have to remember. I can't let it take my mind this time, and I can't let myself "change."

"Damn you, Brock!" she screams. "Damn you for making me remember!"

I keep walking forward in spite of how loud her cries become. Her agony turns into a wall of pain behind me which I can hear growing fainter and fainter. Ahead, the image of the dark sage looms closer as I continue to move. As the distance between us becomes shorter and his image grows larger, I can hear the voices of different people throughout my life echoing within my mind. I can recall conversations between those who used to be in charge of me when I was a much younger soldier, and I can recall almost every conversation I've ever had with Kalina and Alina.

Their voices keep getting louder as the face of the smiling sage gets clearer.

I make it to the room at the end of the connecting chambers to stand before the Ajalu. Its gaze remains unbroken as it stares back at me, and it retains a condescending, creepy smile that's been there from the start. It watched all of my comrades die, drew the demon, Ekikon, out of me, and then it made Ein have a mental breakdown. It made me forget what I'd done to make it this far and how I lost all of my equipment in doing so, but I'll force it to remind me.

As I step toward the sage with clenched fists, it looks up at me with black holes for eyes, then it gives off a black light which pushes me back a few steps.

"Shit," I shake off my nervousness, then I step forward again.

The sage's empty eye sockets blink once, then a stone hand reaches out of the ground to grab my left leg; it blinks twice, and another hand reaches up to grab my right.

The images of Ixilho and the stabbing Ajalu appear in front of me. The knife-wielding Ajalu rushes to my side and stabs me three times in the stomach. As it laughs, three open wounds gush with blood, and I start to scream. I panic, and I punch out at the Ajalu, but my fists pass through air.

When I look down again, my wounds aren't there anymore.

The image of Ixilho walks up to my left side and dashes me across the head with his metal pillar. He dashes me again and again, and my skulls feels like it's being crushed into pieces by each blow. When I cry out in pain and touch my scalp, my hands feel nothing but unbroken skin.

The meditating Ajalu cackles with wicked laughter and says to me, **"They and the wounds they inflict aren't real, but your Imago isn't good enough to know that. Let's change them a little bit."**

It snaps its fingers: Kalina appears on my left, still holding the pillar, and Alina appears on my right, wielding two knives.

"Wait, Alina—"

I try to stop her, but the image of Alina giggles and thrusts her blades into my side. Kalina beats down on me with her metal pillar, and the sage laughs even harder.

"In this case, I know far too much and you know less than you should. For your entire journey through this place, I've watched you and your comrades suffer. He who survives trauma where others perish suffers to an exponentially greater degree. Kalina and Alina, harbingers of hate and love."

Kalina grabs me by the chin and says, "Remember, what's mine is mine. Your body doesn't belong to you, and, if you think it does—" she smashes the pillar over my head and laughs, "then I'll hit you again."

Alina stabs me once, says, "Daddy, why couldn't you stop it?" She stabs me again and says, "Daddy, why couldn't you cure it and stop it from killing me?" She stabs me a third time, then she says, "Daddy, you don't love me. You let it kill me."

"I didn't let it kill you, honey," I say through tears.

"Shut up!" Kalina screams while bashing me in the head. "You're nothing but a failure, Brock. Don't lie to her!"

"I'm a good father," I shout. I raise my voice even more and yell, "I'm a good father!" I repeat, "I was a good father; I was a good husband—I swear it! I loved them both, and I never gave up! I've never stopped trying, never stopped loving!"

I shout and I shout, and the two images disappear. The sage stops laughing, then it tilts its head to the side and looks as though it feels pity when regarding me again.

"That's what I was waiting for, that expression of grief right there. Human, you've shown me so much pain, so much pain that I have nothing but gratitude. I can see what you cannot. I know how this ends, and thus I have prepared for it.

"You will be my vessel, Brock. I will let you communicate, in part, with those affected by the manipulations of the Mulungus. In place of your Imago, I will let you see into the hearts of those around you and know what grief that they've endured."

"I want no part of you!" I yell, "You're a monster!"

"It is no longer your choice. I will live inside your mind and protect you long enough to savor every moment of grief that I can. This partnership is unavoidable."

"BROCK," I hear Ein shout from behind me, "GET DOWN!"

On instinct, I drop to the floor in time to hear—
—PYTHAGORA: LONGSHOT—

I sense immense power approaching me. My head buzzes and feels hot as something passes over it.

A radiant emerald light, shaped in the likeness of an arrow, beams overhead and blasts into the body of the Ajalu sage. Such power engulfs the Ajalu in a bright emerald flame, and it laughs as its form breaks apart as it's devoured by the bolt of energy.

"I'll see you again, Brock," whispers the sage before its spirit is shredded into wisps of black smoke. I inhale some of these wisps without meaning to upon my next breath, but I don't feel any different from doing so.

Ein approaches from behind and with a pronounced limp while carrying a sniper rifle covered in soot. When I turn around to face her, she confronts me with a bitter look.

"Don't ever ask about my mom again," she says.

12
Stepping Forward

--

Brock

--

EIN LEANS ON ME AS THE TWO OF US MOVE down a dark corridor together. We're the only survivors of our squad, and she looks like she's starting to fade out of consciousness. I can still feel a slight aura coming from her, but that's also beginning to weaken. When I ask if she's okay, she doesn't respond; a few seconds later, however, she nods her head and points forward as she gestures for us to keep moving.

"We're almost there," I say to comfort her, but there's still no response.

The black hallway continues leading down and toward a dark, metal door. From around the door frame, I see light shining in from the other side. This light gives me hope, lets me know that at least one struggle is coming to an end. When I reach the door, I hear it unlatch automatically, and I pass through.

I walk into what looks like a massive hangar, with a plain grey floor and dark, shallow steps leading down from a series of metal doors lining both my side and the wall across from me. As I help Ein balance herself while the two of us descend the steps to the ground below, I notice a large group of recruits gathering near the center of the room. From several of the other doors, I start to see other recruits emerge; some of them walk out while shuddering and clutching their shoulders; others walk out with wide eyes staring straight ahead; still others appear with open wounds and covered in blood.

Survivors, just like me, emerge with injuries they can't hide. Whereas some look forlorn or shellshocked, with stares that gaze far into something I can't see, others shake and talk to themselves on the way to the center. From some doors, recruits carry the bodies of their fallen comrades, and, from others, I can hear the screams of those who've had limbs amputated, the screams of those who might not make it to see the end.

As Ein and I walk toward the center, anyone we pass by eyes us with suspicion. One soldier stops to look me over and says, "I can see that thing in you. You shouldn't have brought it here."

When I ignore him and continue moving, he aims his rifle at my head.

Boom. Another soldier shoots him, spits on his corpse, and walks on while saying, "Crazy bastard. He didn't deserve to make it." Underneath thin, cropped black hair, green eyes stare back at me over a sly smile. He offers me a handshake, and I take it. "Name's Iken Jair. You owe me now."

"I guess so," is my response, and the two of us nod to each other before joining the greater formation up ahead.

In the center of the room, dozens of survivors gather together and begin forming columns of ten and ranks numbering twenty. As Ein and I take a spot next to Iken Jair in the third rank, I hear a mix of cold, dead silence from some next to the frightened complaints of others. I hear groans followed by cursing alongside recruits who tell those complaining to, "Suck it up." Past a few heads to the right, one man shouts at another for crying, and, when that crying doesn't stop, they start throwing hands. The crier has a shoulder injury, and the recruit harassing him digs his finger into that injury, screams, "Fuck you, weakling!" and shoots the crier in the head.

This causes gasps to go up all around, and a group of three other recruits haul off the killer, drag him outside of the formation, and curse his name before shooting him, too.

The voices around me grow louder. Someone in the rear of the formation begins to panic; he shouts, "They're never gonna come for us! It's over—this is all some big fucking joke to them! They'll never co—" another recruit cuts him off with a solid punch to the jaw.

In the midst of complaints, cries of fear, and worried gossip, Ein murmurs, "I wish they would all just shut up."

Up above, two colossal panels of grey metal begin to creak and screech as they part in the middle. A narrow sliver of light beams down onto an elevated platform in front of us, and then the screeching grows louder as both panels start to slide open, revealing sunshine from the surface world.

This harsh noise causes everyone to become quiet and alert, and we all begin to stare up into a new dawn shining down overhead.

Behind the screeching of two opening panels, I hear what sounds like two engines humming in sync as they produce a fluttering which spreads throughout the atmosphere. The panels spread open completely, and then I see what looks like the bottom of two giant, metallic feet descending from above the hangar. Attached to both feet are silver, bulky beams, connected by squared, blocky kneecaps, to even bulkier thighs.

Its thighs descend and give way to the thick frame of a torso surrounded by hundreds of small cables that are wrapped around a massive center. These cables surround its center in what appears to be a spherical shield which winds around an oval cockpit covered in black glass. From both sides of the cockpit, two pairs of silver arms with claw-like hands extend out and around to meet as they clasp together in front of its main body. From behind its torso, two columns of five propulsion jets emit flames that grow weaker as the giant mech suit descends to land on the platform before us. As its jets turn off, its engine cools down to a soft hum; the glass of the cockpit slides upward and then springs open to expose someone seated on a dark, leather chair, with their body connected to a series of smaller cables.

A robust, barrel-chested man with broad shoulders, a thick beard, and grey hair running past his shoulders stands up from the cockpit seat and strides toward us. As he does, I see a green face tattoo of a serpentine dragon exposed more clearly under the light shining down from above and a broad, flat-ended sword strapped to his back. This man reaches inside the pocket of his blue trench coat to take out a small microphone attached to a plastic earpiece. As he fixes it to fit around his right ear, he breathes in deeply, and I see the faint outline of a dark red aura surrounding his body.

He breathes out and his aura explodes around him like a flaming halo. Just outside of his aura, I catch a brief glimpse of what looks like a complex sign or character belonging to a language I've never heard nor seen; the presence of his zol speaks to a unique kind of strength, one I didn't pick up on when I was around Horokaida. He takes another deep breath, then he begins to explain.

"I am General Zamolock, the most important member of your current chain of command who you'll ever meet. To you, I am God. If you've made it this far, that makes you my children—scratch that—that makes you "chosen," special.

"For this training exercise, we sent in at least four hundred and fifty recruits on what we'll call a little survival run. This was our latest experiment, and we've finished with a little under two hundred of you. We began with nine sergeants, and we ended with only one. Compared to our last test run, we'll call this a 'success,' but you won't understand why until I tell you the reason for all the suffering you've endured.

"Operation Echo-14 will be our first official attempt at taking the fight to Alandra. Because Enrec no longer has access to sentinels, we've had to rethink our strategy with regard to the enemies surrounding us. Our country is vulnerable, and the rest of the world knows it; therefore, people like me are the only ones left who can guide our forces to victory. That is why I am your God, and, from here on out, you will place your trust completely in the plans that have been laid out for you. If you stop to question what's happening, you'll be left behind, like those who weren't capable of making it this far.

"Our nation once had a series of forward operating bases scattered across the surface above us. When war continued to break out between Avva's Republic and Alandra, we lost a lot of good people. With loss, there comes failure; with failure, there is grief. Something fed off this grief, and you can call this 'thing' the Mulungus that sits high in the sky as we speak.

"Alandra has sided with demons, partnering with several clans stationed South of this area, and the Mulungus above is one hell of an anathema. This Mulungus is precisely why we had all of you participate in this training exercise, and it's because that abomination in the sky might just hold the secret to us winning what will be the riskiest operation we've ever engaged in.

"Hundreds of you died, and yet hundreds of you made it through in spite of the challenges the spawn of the Mulungus presented. Enrec believes that those who survive encounters with its spawn will be better prepared to handle the demons blocking our paths to settlements within Alandran territory. Thus, fighting the Mulungus has made you all mean as shit; because of what you've been through, nothing will hold you back from totally annihilating the enemy. No challenge will be too great, and no order will be impossible.

"Because of what you've survived, you are the greatest warriors alive. You were destined to destroy Alandra, and even that dark abomination knows it. Now's the time to place full faith in Avva, full faith in the Republic. Enrec has taken you from 'strong' to unstoppable, and so, my children, let us go forth and fight to honor those who died in your place. Let us meet demons where they feel the most comfortable and shatter their resolves. Let us fight and never stop fighting, not until we've become the ultimate warriors of this great country. All of you will be inducted as special operatives of Enrec, and all of you will live on to be regarded as the strongest fighters who ever lived. Soldiers, are you with me?"

The entire formation shouts, "Yes Sir!"

As the giant mech projects the flag and colors of the Republic of Avva, General Zamolock screams, "Then let's go! Sing the national anthem, sing it loud and proud, warriors!"

The colossal mech plays the song of our country, which rings through a hangar filled with those of us who've braved some of the worst traumas anyone could ever endure. We stand together, as one unit, and we all start to sing. In spite of the pain, my memory of all the events leading up to this point begin to fade without my control. They fade, and all I know is that I made it to the end, to graduation from a brief onslaught of oppression.

--

Follow orders. Always follow orders. From day one, since the time I was an infant, I've been controlled and commanded by someone else.

I thought that I was my own person. In serving what I always believed was the "greatest country in the world," I thought that I would realize myself through service. I served without complaint, and I suffered what felt like endless agony as the years passed me by. I always envied Tavon. I hated him, and now I understand where this hatred comes from.

I can't remember what happened in those tunnels. I can't remember what I faced or how I fought them or how I even survived; it's like I wasn't supposed to survive in the first place. From the beginning, maybe I was never supposed to make it. Within me, there lives "The Guardian," and I think that he's always been there. From now on, now that he's been given more control and power than ever before, I'll go to the battlefield alongside him. What I can't face, he can. When he disappears, I become myself again, but I can only realize myself when I no longer simply follow commands as they're given.

When I follow orders, I am "Brock," a child of war. Without those orders, I am nothing.

Maybe, just maybe, it's time for me to become something.

TO BE CONTINUED...

Note From The Author

Due to recent events, I've had to cut *Volume Five* much shorter than I ever intended. Unfortunately, flashdrives containing a significant portion of *Volume Five* were stolen from me, and so, to avoid having to rewrite the first sixty or so pages because someone might upload content which is my own, I've decided to go ahead and publish what I've been able to write. In between moving States, finishing a degree, and transferring to a new postsecondary institution, it's been difficult to work at the pace to which I'm accustomed. As a result of these changes, this short work could be considered the "beta version" of *Volume Five*. What's most likely going to happen is that I'll be uploading a Second Edition of *Volume Five*, and this Second Edition will contain everything that I intended to be included in this volume of the series. If this plan isn't chosen, however, I will simply incorporate what I haven't here into *Volume Six*. At this moment, I'm at an impasse. Fortunately, there is still a massive amount of content left to be written. In the end, I feel as though it will one day be appropriate to combine every volume of *Angelos Odyssey* into one book, which was how I intended it to be read all along. This is going to be a long ride, so I appreciate everyone who's had the patience to stick it out with me.

Sincerely,
Josh